Amelia Garland Mears

# Mercia

The Astronomer Royal

Amelia Garland Mears

**Mercia**
*The Astronomer Royal*

ISBN/EAN: 9783337347550

Printed in Europe, USA, Canada, Australia, Japan

Cover: Foto ©Andreas Hilbeck / pixelio.de

More available books at **www.hansebooks.com**

# MERCIA,

## THE ASTRONOMER ROYAL:

### A Romance.

BY

## A. GARLAND MEARS,

AUTHOR OF

'IDYLLS, LEGENDS, AND LYRICS,' THE STORY OF A TRUST,'
'TALES OF OUR TOWN,' ETC.

LONDON:

SIMPKIN, MARSHALL, HAMILTON, KENT & CO. LTD.

4 STATIONERS'-HALL COURT.

1895.

PRINTED BY
SPOTTISWOODE AND CO., NEW-STREET SQUARE
LONDON

# MERCIA

## THE ASTRONOMER ROYAL.

'Whoever knows the origin, the entrance, the locality, and the five-fold power of life enjoys immortality.'

From THE PRASNA, in *Bibliotheca Indica*.

# CONTENTS

## PROLOGUE.



## MERCIA, THE ASTRONOMER ROYAL.

# PROLOGUE

## PART I

THE year of grace, 2002, had arrived and the world had seen many changes. The kingdoms of the earth had gone through great experiences. Nations had risen and fallen; the boundaries of Empires had been modified; for a serious redistribution of territory had taken place.

Petty sovereignties had now become merged into greater ones, having fallen a prey to the strong; for the dominant Powers had divided the spoil by agreement.

Nevertheless, on the whole, peace and contentment reigned; for advanced knowledge, not only taught the inutility, gross inhumanity, and waste of war, but science had made such wonderful progress in the arts of warfare throughout the whole world, that a battle actually meant the complete annihilation of both sides ; thus a victory for either became an impossibility.

Along with this enforced peace-keeping the wave of civilisation had spread everywhere carrying its mind-culture, its arts, and handicrafts to the uttermost parts of the earth ; until the world had become a huge beehive of active industry, although not necessarily a severe muscle-wearing one.

Through all the generations dating from the close of the nineteenth century the social question relative to the status of woman had been ever uppermost, having been kept to the front by the intense longing of the sex for a wider walk of life, a more extended field of action.

They demanded a great reformation, a complete recast of social economics.

The leading features of their programme being a higher education, which should be recognised by the Universities, Law, and Medical Corporations, in order that more honourable, lucrative, and responsible employments might be opened to them.

They demanded also, political, social, and marital equality between the sexes ; for they averred that women were being cramped and crippled by old-time conventionalities, the outcome of the customs and prejudices of mediæval ignorance and tyranny, which had invariably relegated their sex to a lower platform of liberty.

As citizens it placed them in the position of minors and lunatics, they averred, and as wives it gave them but little more authority than what their children possessed from a legal point of view, however talented and cultivated they might be.

Loud and bitter were the railings of the dominant sex against the movement. Men scoffed and derided ' the new woman,' as they mockingly termed her.

She became the subject of epigram, pun, and pleasantry generally ; the butt of every shallow humorist, and dubbed ' the new darn on the old bluestocking,' whatever that might mean. She was told that her aspirations were bold and offensive in the extreme ; that they ' unsexed ' her.

Nor was she spared by her own sex. If

a lady novelist had the courage to make a stand for social purity the critics would pounce upon her, condemning her work as ' improper.'

Mostly those following this calling were males; but there were to be found feminine monstrosities among writers, who to curry favour with the multitude, stooped to the unworthiness of writing down those devoted champions of liberty for their own sex.

It was a long battle and a hard, this struggle for equality. Man's dominance and woman's subjugation had not been a healthy influence throughout the ages, for either sex.

Society taught, and the laws of the realm favoured the theory, that the code of morality for the man was widely different to that which should guide the woman.

But the new woman saw whence this incongruity sprang, and showed that it had its birth and continued existence in the coarser instincts of the male, whose desires it tended to foster and encourage.

' Truly,' she exclaimed, ' the arrogance and selfishness of man is not difficult to discover, although veiled by the hypocritical excuse of keeping intact the sweet delicacy and spirituality of woman. Men demand that we should continue to repose a child-like confidence in their goodness; well, we shall be only too ready to grant it as soon as we are assured that they have made themselves worthy of our trust.'

Education and experience had now opened her eyes : impelled by necessity she shook off the bonds that had bound her so long and utilised the talents that had for ages lain dormant, turning them into worthier and more useful channels.

How their first steps in the ways of liberty were derided! Nevertheless, there came forward high-souled men who held out a helping hand to these struggling children, who were laboriously and anxiously stretching and straining to reach the longed-for goal.

The crowning joy came at last. Slowly, and by almost imperceptible degrees, she won one concession, and then another, until by the time the second millenary was reached her great ambition was attained.

Like all wise reforms it benefited equally its adversaries as supporters; and man, who at the outset bitterly opposed the movement, reaped the advantage derived therefrom, to his own comfort and content.

Woman's position was now assured, and she took her place alongside man on equal terms. If a post of honour, or high emolument were vacant, sex was not taken into consideration in the choice of a candidate, for the person best suited for the position was selected according to his or her proved ability, or past experience.

It frequently happened that a young fellow earning but 100*l.* a year would woo successfully a young lady filling a position of importance that yielded her 500*l.* per annum. For it might chance that she had enjoyed the advantage over him of a superior training, or inherited abler ability for that particular employment; and these combined with perhaps, superior family influence exerted on her behalf had given her the better start.

In such a case as this, with their united incomes, the young couple were in a position to set up housekeeping in a fairly respectable style; the bridegroom's good luck might be envied by his companions, but no one thought the worse of either.

Moreover it worked beneficially for the male in other ways. If accident, or sickness deprived a man of the capability of following his employment, he and his family, were not reduced to want, for the wife became the bread-winner, leaving him in charge of the housekeeping.

This arrangement was considered no hardship by the wife; for she was relieved of domestic cares, and control of domestic servants, which, as a rule, the husband discharged with great success. It was frequently found that a master obtained readier obedience and more faithful service than a mistress. Whether this was owing to his requirements being less exacting than those of a mistress, or to that indefinable influence which one sex holds over the other, cannot be determined; doubtless it was a combination of the two that gave the man greater empire over the woman-servant.

It is not to be supposed that a domestic servant occupied the humble position she held in previous times; for a well-appointed household requiring at least four servants, in the nineteenth century would at this period

need but one. The vast amount of mechanical
contrivances worked by electricity minimised
labour to such an extent that it raised the
position of a domestic servant to that of a
working electrician of the nineteenth century;
which period saw the birth of the practical
use of electric energy. In fact, a thoroughly
good domestic servant who knew her work,
that is to say, a woman who understood, and
successfully conducted the various machines,
keeping them in working order, could readily
command her two pounds a week, and run a
home, husband, and children on her own
account.

The social economy of this time was
entirely different to that of any previous
period. Marriage in no way incapacitated a
woman-servant from keeping her situation.
Indeed, it had a contrary effect; most people
preferring a steady-going married woman
with responsibilities, to a flirty inexperienced
maiden who might use her position in the
household to wile away a heedless son, or a
somewhat lonesome husband. As a rule,
however, such an occurrence happened rarely;
the marriage state was mostly a very happy

one, and faithfully kept on both sides, for a high standard of morality ruled supreme.

Other factors supported this beneficent condition; for all being equal as bread-winners, and the number of the sexes equally balanced, a man deemed himself fortunate when he secured a good wife and did his utmost to please her.

On her side affection alone prompted her to marry; the unworthy motive of making marriage the means of obtaining a home of her own, no longer existed, as every parent trained his daughter equally as his son to hold a position of independence, by giving her a trade, or profession to follow.

Both humble and high-born possessed more or less practical knowledge of physi-ology; especially those branches dealing directly with health, and the functions of reproduction, which enabled women to fill more intelligently the positions of wife and mother.

It was appointed by Government that all persons should be taught the more important branches of this science in the public schools, as soon as they reached the age of twelve

years together with the principles of social
economy. It was considered a gross immorality on the part of parents to bring into
existence a large family of children, whom
they could not possibly rear with comfort to
themselves, or with any degree of justice to
their offspring.

But over and above the personal inconvenience of poor people being overburdened
with children, the disadvantage of giving
birth to large families was recognised by all
from an economic point of view: for the
world was becoming so thickly populated
that it appeared obvious a difficulty would
arise in providing foodstuffs for so many
millions of human beings, notwithstanding
the very material assistance the science of
chemistry afforded in feeding the multitude.

All persons, therefore recognised the necessity of supporting legislative authority on
this point, for being an intellectual people
they saw it worked to their advantage from
every point of view.

Inordinate reproduction interfered with a
wife's ability to supplement her husband's income by following her own profession, and

thereby making a very narrow income into an easy one.

In bygone days if the mistress of a public school entered the marriage state she entered the schoolroom no more; custom decreed that with marriage all bread winning ceased on her side, and her husband's small income must suffice.

Of course the *raison d'être* of this custom was not far to seek, for her child-bearing duties, to which no limit was placed, would considerably interfere with those of her situation.

But at this advanced period public opinion decreed that such a course was the outcome of brute ignorance; for physiological and psychological science taught that the position of parent was the most responsible in all creation, and to bring any number of children into the world until Nature refused to do more, was a condition of life in its wildest state; for man in every other form of life controls the exuberance of Nature, for wise purposes.

As soon as a wife decided on becoming a mother,—and most women looked forward to

that position with keen interest, for the love
of children is ever paramount in the female
breast,—she would brace herself to the fulfilment of the duties of this great responsibility.

She realised that on herself alone rested,
not only the building up of the physical
frame of her unborn child, but also the for-
mation of the pre-natal mind, with all its
mental and moral capacities.

She knew that every thought, impulse,
and action of hers would leave their impress upon the brain of her child; for a
stimulus would be given to the development
of the faculties in those directions, according to the degree in which she exercised her
own.

In order, therefore to ensure herself the
possession of a child perfect in physique, and
intellect; and endowed with such faculties of
mind as formed her beau ideal of a beautiful
character, she underwent a course of self-
denial and watchfulness throughout the whole
period of pregnancy.

During this important period, the greatest
in her life, she took heed that no emotion,

thought, or action was indulged in on her part that she would object to seeing reproduced in her child, however modified these might be by the new individuality.

To ensure this she followed a system of wholesome and healthy employment, which served the two-fold purpose of keeping her mind pure, and her muscle-power in practice. By experience it was found that the most beautiful characters had been given to the world by parents noted for their industry, morality and unselfishness.

Then there were the intellectual powers of the child's mind to consider, for it was not left to chance the arrangement of his talents, or capabilities for a profession.

Expectant parents took time by the forelock, for instead of waiting for the period when their son's schooling would be completed for the choice of a profession, they carefully considered the question long before he put in an appearance, and made their plans regarding his future with twentieth-century forethought.

If it so happened that the ambition of a couple was to see their son a professor of music then the mother-that-was-to-be took her *rôle* accordingly.

During this interesting time she would devote herself almost exclusively to the pursuit of music; daily practising on the instruments she wished him to excel in; studying the theory of music, attending high-class musical entertainments; encouraging lovers of music at her house, and in fact, neglecting nothing that lay in her power to foster and encourage the growth of that group of faculties, whose possession makes the perfect musician.

Indeed, the friends of a lady *enceinte* would suspect her condition, not from seeing her lying about on the couch, or other indolent indulgences, but from her increased activities in a regular and definite direction.

'It's easy to see,' a neighbour would remark in fireside parlance, 'that Mistress Woodward is expecting a son; evidently they are going to make him a civil engineer. Mark, how she is slaving over mathematics and reading up every work on engineering she can lay her hands on. Why, her boudoir is filled with mechanical drawings: you would think she was about building all the suspension bridges, and electrometers in the Empire.  It is a son, you may be sure; she would hardly put a daughter to such a profession, seeing that when one comes she will be an heiress.  Yes, the grandmother left all her property to the granddaughter, *when she arrives.*  I suppose they will have one; it goes without saying that they will, *under the circumstances.*'

Or this might be the gossip.

' It's coming off at last!  They're going to give themselves a baby—poor things!  'Twas a silly love match, thou remembers, and their united incomes were as nothing compared with their ideas, brought up as they were in every luxury.  However, the wife got a good appointment last October owing to the influence of her friends ; result—she is going to have a baby—a girl, I am told.  It is plain enough to see what trade the child is to follow, for the expectant mother is now running a laboratory and slaves in it nightly, besides attending the Government lectures on chemistry held weekly in the large hall of the Science Schools.  Well, it is a useful pro-

fession, and will do equally well for a boy;
it's just possible they may have made a mistake and the baby will prove to be a boy
after all.  I never thought either of them
over intelligent—they are sure to blunder—
but what matters it?  They can have a girl
next time.  Of course they will treat themselves to two children—they can now afford it.'

Still another sample of twentieth century
table talk.

*Mr. Brown.*    'Hast thou seen Smithers
lately?  It is a long time since I set eyes on
him; what is he doing?'

*Mr. White.*    'Oh, all his spare time is
taken up showing Mistress Smithers how to
manufacture flying machines.  He takes her
into his workshop daily, explaining the uses
of this, that and the other.  She has a lathe
of her own, run by electricity, and she makes
the parts and fits them together.  Of course
as soon as the baby is born she will drop it,
for Smithers is well off now; capital business
that flying machine one, especially with that
new patent of his—it almost goes like the
wind, and a lot steadier.'

*Mr. Brown.*    'Bless my life!  why she

went through all that fag four years ago, I remember very well I could never get a minute with him. As soon as ever his workmen were gone, in went the wife for her lessons, and mighty quick she was too, in taking it all in. Are they going to have *two* sons?'

*Mr. White.* 'Not if they know it! They made a mistake last time; it appears 'twas an order for a daughter that went, while they thought it was for a son, so Mistress Smithers has to go through all her exercises *de novo*; it is to be hoped they have made no blunder *this* time, for it is no joke after all, for the poor woman.'

*Mr. Brown.* 'The boy should be a genius when he comes, seeing that *both* parents are adepts in the business. Occasionally we have freaks of nature,—now, haven't we? Rememberest thou those Percys, they were going to have a *poet*, forsooth! but, ha, ha, ha, he turned out a simpleton!! He now takes the pence for the man who lends out his flying machine to boys. So much for manufacturing poets beforehand.'

*Mr. White.* 'It was a maxim of the ancients that poets must be born not made.

and it still holds good in these days of light : for a great poet only comes once in an epoch. He is an intellectual giant, as it were, and the conditions under which he is formed are not yet fathomed. It is comparatively easy for a woman to take up any ordinary employment with a view of giving a certain bias to the child's faculties, but how in the name of goodness can a person all at once simulate the poet, and expect her child to come into the world a ready-made bard—why it is preposterous ! '

*Mr. Brown.* ' We cannot limit the possibilities of the future :  only a hundred years ago the possibility of arranging the sex of a child was laughed at as a simple absurdity. Now we arrange not only the number of our children but their sex also ; and very properly too, for we can do greater justice to our progeny when we know what we are about, than if they came by blind chance, merely.'

*Mr. White.* ' We are twenty-first century people, now—let us remember that fact, two thousand and two ! Yea, verily, the world is growing very old and that blessed millennium hasn't come yet ! '

*Mr. Brown.* ' *This* is the millennium. We shall get no better. Is not the prophecy fulfilled of the ancient poets—" The wolf and the lamb shall lie down together? " Where is war? It has ceased to exist. Civilisation and science have worked out the miracle, and given to war its quietus.'

It is necessary to explain that by this time such a perfect knowledge of physiology was attained that the sex of the desired offspring could be regulated by parents. As soon as the discovery was made, and fully and completely tested, it was not locked up as a professional secret, but was given to the people by order of the Government in a handbook of health that was issued yearly at a nominal cost, which contained up-to-date information on hygiene, or general management of Health, and Home. By this means at least two-thirds of the children born were males, which kept the balance fairly even of the sexes. For notwithstanding the fact that Nature had at all times given the predominance of number to the masculine sex, yet owing to the numerous accidents that befell men while in the pursuit of their calling; and also to the severer strain on their constitution as the breadwinners, the mortality was consequently greater. From these causes mainly the nations found themselves mostly, with a redundance of adult females.

But a complete metamorphosis had now set in, for the people had eagerly taken advantage of the information afforded them, availing themselves of it to such an extent that the succeeding generation of males found themselves with a very inadequate supply of wives.

This awkward dilemma was, however, remedied in course of time, and eventually a fairly even number of the sexes was obtained.

But there was still another factor that assisted in maintaining the balance — the opening of trades and professions to women, which custom had kept so long closed against them, causing parents to hesitate in sending their daughters to learn trades and professions. 'Better have no daughters at all,' thought many susceptible ones, 'if they must toil for their living like men.' But time works wonders: the day came when a daughter brought as much honour and credit to her family as ever a son could possibly have achieved.

What men in the first instance regarded as an invasion of their rights, proved in the end an inestimable blessing. A wife ceased to be a kind of encumbrance upon a struggling man, and became a helpmate in a very substantial sense; for marriage no longer incapacitating a woman from continuing her employment, the income of a couple was doubled : by this means the two were enabled to live in greater comfort and with less strain and worry to the husband. Thus the longevity of the male was increased by the more equal distribution of labour between the sexes, for the wear and tear to the nervous system in the battle of life being reduced, had its share in prolonging masculine life and sustaining an equality of number of the sexes.

As every person loved his profession, or trade, 'being born to it,' in a most literal sense, his enthusiasm and interest in it never slackened, consequently, no woman deemed it a hardship to follow the calling her parents had designed for her, even when marriage made it no longer a necessity. When the duties of her situation were discharged each day, supposing she filled one, for few women ever thought of throwing up a good post on account of getting married—she would return to her home, whose appointments denoted the presence of the greatest refinement and comfort, and finish the day, for the hours of labour were short, in the society of her husband and children, varied by the enjoyment of social pleasures, or intellectual pursuits.

## PART II

FOR over a hundred years woman had been gradually developing in strength and stature. and had by this time attained as great a height as man formerly possessed. 'Woman's weakness' was an unknown term, except from ancient literature, for owing to the various athletic exercises which for generations had been the universal custom for girls and women to engage in, and also to the increased physical strength attained by abstemiousness from much child-bearing, they had almost overtaken the males in vigour, and endurance. Courage being the accompaniment of bodily strength the myth of a woman running away from a mouse was regarded as a silly invention of their ancestors for the purpose of pleasantry, or a playful manner of showing up the difference of the organisation of the sexes. But there were cynics to be found who averred that the comic papers of the nineteenth century in their skits on society gave as true a reflection of its condition, from one point of view, as the most veracious and trustworthy historian could have afforded.

It appeared, indeed, utterly absurd to the twentieth-century mind, when they turned over the leaves of some ancient copy of *Punch* to see the joke portraying the bald-headed pater looking aghast when the monthly nurse presents him with the twelfth consignment, which are twins !

'Why the man ought to be dandling his grandchildren at his time of life, he is actually bald, and babies coming still!' the reader of those ancient cynicisms would exclaim.

They could not understand the imprudence of parents bringing children into the world for almost the whole of their natural lives. Leaving themselves without leisure or ease to enjoy the fruits of their industry in middle age, while yet youthful enough to appreciate the pleasures of life.

The nursery story—most artistically illustrated, of course,—descriptive of the condition of their ancestors formed a curious revelation to twentieth-century children.

'This is the man who toiled all day to fill

the mouths of seven hungry children that didn't get enough.

'This is the woman all worn with care, who was wife to the man that toiled all day, to fill the mouths of seven hungry children that didn't get enough.

'This is the strap the woman used, all worn with care, who was wife to the man that toiled all day to fill the mouths of seven hungry children that didn't get enough.

'This is the pup that eat up the strap the woman used, all worn with care, who was wife to the man that toiled all day to fill the mouths of seven hungry children that didn't get enough.

'This is the cat that clawed the pup, that eat up the strap, the woman used, all worn with care, who was wife to the man that toiled all day to fill the mouths of seven hungry children that didn't get enough.

'This is the tank that drowned the cat, that clawed the pup, that eat up the strap the woman used, all worn with care, who was wife to the man that toiled all day to fill the mouths of seven hungry children that didn't get enough.'

This melancholy record of the fortunes of the nineteenth century representative peasant, was doubtless a variation of the legend of the old woman that lived in a shoe. Nevertheless it amused the little tots of twenty-first century time. For the extraordinary picture of seven little children inhabiting one poor little cottage appeared utterly absurd to their advanced minds, which could scarcely comprehend the folly of a poor man possessing more mouths to fill than was possible. 'What did he want with all those?' they innocently inquired.

But their nurse could only reply—'She didn't quite know: it was a way they had in nineteenth-century times.'

The laws of health were so strictly taught in all schools that no individual could possibly grow up ignorant on those points; and every man, mostly, knew how to take charge of his own body.

Nevertheless professors of medicine still flourished on the face of the earth; but the masculine sex had for generations past lost the monopoly of the profession.

As a rule, however, the lady doctor was

in no greater demand than her male rival, men still holding their own to some extent; for the world will ever see those women who prefer men to dance attendance on them.

The profession was, indeed, pretty equally divided between the sexes; most mothers preferring females to prescribe for their children in times of dangerous sickness, believing that they were more successful in their treatment of the troubles of childhood. Besides, it followed as a natural consequence that as the lady accoucheur brought the child into the world, which was the invariable custom, it was only fair that she should have the medical care of the little one afterwards.

The serious infant mortality which prevailed among the lower orders up to the close of the nineteenth century, was now so reduced, that parents, as a rule, succeeded in rearing their families intact.

Greater enlightenment in the methods of their upbringing, together with superior sanitary arrangements of the domicile, no doubt tended largely towards effecting this change.

Small families being the rule, instead of the exception, it must be admitted that with a lesser number to provide for, greater care and comfort could be bestowed upon their offspring; so that the reduction of the birth-rate had the effect of reducing the death-rate ; this fact combined with increased longevity of the adult, quite doubled the average of human life.

The difference in dress between men and women was not great ; the sexes were mostly distinguishable by the method of dressing their hair.

Men had ceased cutting their hair closely, for it was found that this practice materially injured its growth, and finally ended in making all the males bald before they were twenty years of age.

Specialists averred that the cause of the trouble arose from two sources. By constantly cropping the hair an unnatural stimulus was imparted to its growth, which quickly impoverished the hair follicles, and so brought about their early decay. Also, the scalp being unduly deprived of its natural covering of long hair was left an easy prey to every germ, or fungus that chose to make its home there. For these reasons men decided to wear their hair long, and usually kept it from six to twelve inches in length, in curls about their neck, which had the effect of giving them a very romantic appearance.

Women allowed their hair its full natural length, arranging it in coils and plaits, pretty much in the manner of the ancients.

At this time there were persons with fads who affected high art in gastronomical matters ; preferring to patronise the food-chemist rather than the butcher and baker. Chemical food-stuffs for the supply of the waste of the various tissues of the body were arranged in pills and tabloids, the quantity allowed for a meal being printed on the label.

This practice however, failed to meet with anything approaching popular favour, for mankind still loved too well the pleasures of the table to give up a good dinner for a pill. For who would prefer a nitrogenous tabloid to the delicacies of the banquet, which form the necessary concomitants of the soul-in-spiring nectars usually quaffed by the appreciative Teuton on every available occasion ?

Indeed, to him the loss of the sensations of that comfort and satisfaction which follow a good meal was tantamount to bidding adieu to the most substantial pleasure of life.

Besides, their internal arrangements had something to say in the matter; and their utter collapse for want of some substance to keep them in position proved a warning to the daring experimenter.

Notwithstanding all the arguments of advanced scientists, the food-chemists failed in disestablishing the old-fashioned system of eating and drinking.

Moreover there were physiologists who declared that it was an impossibility as man is constituted, to sustain life by means of elemental substances being introduced into the system unless a complete reconstruction of the organisation could be effected.

For the various organs that acted together, forming a laboratory for the change of food-stuffs into vital force, having no occupation must necessarily languish, and get out of gear through sheer inanition.

Thus the revolution in animal economy was perforce left over for the people of a more advanced period to deal with.

# PART III

THE nineteenth century saw the development of natural science to such a gigantic extent that the people could only exclaim—'It is like reading a fairy tale of double-distilled enchantment; Aladdin's lamp is as nothing compared with it!'

Great as was the civilisation of the ancients their genius had never attained to such heights as were reached by the scientists of that epoch.

Electricity was impounded into the service of man, and put to every possible purpose.

Experiment and research continued to be the order of the day; and the great glow of enthusiasm that fired the votaries of science never abated until all that was possible to be learnt concerning the adaptations of electric energy were known far and wide. Before the dawn of the twentieth century every country on the face of the earth was bound together by a network of electrical energy.

Scientific knowledge had therefore made such vast progress all over the world, and the uses to which electric force could be applied had become so widely known that nations found they must settle their differences by some method other than warfare.

By the use of electric lightning, as it was named, to distinguish it from cloud lightning, whole armies could be annihilated by a couple of electricians.　And as skilful workmen of this class were in full force in every country, and at the word of command were ready to apply this deadly instrument of destruction with instantaneous effect, the powers of warfare were pretty equally balanced.

In course of time, on this account, standing armies were abolished, for obviously, they were absolutely useless for the defence of a nation, and in their stead a supreme Court of Justice was set up, entitled THE WORLD'S TRIBUNAL.

This was composed of delegates, or representatives from every nation, each being entitled to send two persons who were usually chosen from the ministry.

It is needless to explain that such a position of responsibility was given only to men of excellent wisdom and proved ability, who had already won the confidence of their country. As a rule, the decisions of this unique Court were abided by, but if a judgment gave general dissatisfaction, then a return to an extremely primitive method of warfare was permitted, under certain modified conditions.

A company of picked men, famous in athletic exercises were selected by the countries in dispute and pitted against each other, armed with electrically-charged lances, very short, and silvered over to give them a more imposing appearance.

The object of each combatant was not to take life, or give serious injury to his adversary, but simply to temporarily paralyse his right arm, the combat being conducted according to certain stringent regulations and conditions.

At one time females offered themselves for the trial, and gave good proof of their prowess and ability ; but this ambition did not obtain for long, and their desire of emulation in merely muscular exercises grew into disfavour; for woman considered it incumbent upon her to keep in advance of man in intellectual and philanthropical pursuits.

Social history had taught her that man must possess an ideal for his guidance, and where was that to be found if not in woman? It was her influence, and her example which had advanced him to his present high morality, his present plane of purity.

Sometimes several generations would pass away before an occasion arose for the GREAT TEST TOURNAMENT to take place, so that when an engagement of this kind came off, it formed, in truth, a world's fête. Kings and commoners flocked from all parts to witness this unusual spectacle: for the old love of combativeness was still dominant in the human mind, although mainly kept under excellent restraint.

The opportunity therefore, of seeing such an important contest, the result of which bore such serious issues, was eagerly sought by all classes, in every country. Indeed, it was patronised to such an extent that it was found necessary to restrict the number of sightseers to one million. For it was found most inconvenient to entertain and provide accommodation for more, there being no room for such a heavy addition to their numbers in the already well-filled city. All cities were pretty nearly alike, in this respect, the world being very thickly populated.

The Great Test Tournament formed, in truth, a grand and imposing spectacle. What an exciting scene would then present itself!

Flying machines impelled by electric energy darkened the air. Sumptuous carriages set in motion by the same force, and filled with gaily costumed men and women eager to witness the scene, whirled along the roads formed of cement as smooth as glass, and hard as adamant.

Horsemen elegantly attired, cantered briskly along the side road, which was devoted specially to their use, for that designed for general purposes was too smooth for the equestrian.

Horses, indeed, were trotted out more for display than absolute use, by the wealthy, for the means of locomotion was accessible to all.

The poorest person, almost, could conveniently run his own electric car; for the expense of construction was light, and by a simple process of the conservation of energy the supply of electric force was sustained at a small cost.

By this time the concentration and conservation of solar energy was in general practice; usually large manufactories favoured its use, for the storage of the sun's rays had become practicable and was superseding electricity to some extent. The ocean was no impediment to personal locomotion, for seas were skimmed over by means of electrical flying machines; while ships impelled by the same force were used chiefly for the transport of cargo.

Nevertheless, there was still a large percentage of persons who preferred riding the wave on an electric, or solar energy impelled vessel, to floating through the air in a flying machine, for nerves were not yet out of fashion.

Notwithstanding all the dreams of nineteenth-century political reformers England had still retained its old institutions, for the Empire continued to be ruled by a monarchical form of government diluted somewhat with the constitutional. So far from being a great Republic by this time the tendency went the other way, for new conditions sprang up which gave the Sovereign a degree of absolutism which the fondest hopes of the Royalist could never have conjured up. By reason of marriages and intermarriages between the Royal Houses of Great Britain and Germany the two families became so intermixed that in consequence of the sudden death of the heir-apparent to the German crown, followed immediately by the death of the Emperor, the Sovereign of England woke up one morning to find himself the direct successor to the throne of the Fatherland.

It happened in this way. A great war broke out between Germany and France in the year 1930, and in the midst of a fierce contest, where the great field pieces were charged with missiles which emitted volleys of electric lightning into the German ranks, a French electrician sent an electric bolt at the Emperor and his son, killing the younger royal warrior instantly, and severely injuring the elder. The following day the Emperor succumbed to his injuries, to the intense grief of all his subjects.

This *coup* failed to give the French nation the victory, but it gave the German crown to the Sovereign of England, who was the only successor. This was the last battle Europe ever saw; public opinion decreed that such cruel slaughter should be discontinued for all time. As a matter of course there was much opposition at the outset to the Sovereign of another country swaying the sceptre of their beloved fatherland, albeit he was in reality more German than English.

Long speeches were made in the Reichstag, and ancient laws raked up to show its utter unconstitutional character. But when it was pointed out by their favourite minister, an old man full of wisdom and experience, what a splendid gain it would prove to their country in having such a powerful nation as the English merged into theirs; for united the two could defy the world independently of any alliance with other great Powers. To this unanswerable argument the opposition succumbed, and gracefully gave way to the inevitable.

The two countries set apart a whole week for national rejoicings at this glorious union of two great nations in a manner unparalleled in all history. It was poetically entitled the marriage of the beautiful Sea-Girt Isle with the strong and Ever-Enduring Fatherland. This euphemism took away the bitterness of the pill that most of the Germans were mouthing, for they were not altogether satisfied at seeing their country come under the dominance of another Power, albeit the ties of consanguinity and policy bound both together. But the strongest factor in producing satisfaction was the intense pleasure they felt in arousing the ire and deep indignation of the French nation. who saw at a glance her utter incapacity to cope with a rival whose dominions would now all but encircle her, and whose power and possessions extended to every part of the globe.

Thus it came to pass that Albert Felicitas, King of Great Britain and Ireland, and Emperor of India and Africa, was crowned Emperor of Germany, which now held the small sovereignties of Denmark and Sweden.

Henceforward this great portion of European territory was named THE TEUTONIC EMPIRE, which comprising the Germanic and British Empires united the scattered Teutons into one solid body.

# MERCIA, THE ASTRONOMER ROYAL,

## A ROMANCE.

## CHAPTER I

Long before this period the women of England had become celebrated for their mental attainments, splendid physique, and exceeding beauty; but chiefest of all was the lovely and accomplished Mercia.

Owing to her superior attainments in natural science, but especially that branch dealing with astronomy she was appointed the position of Astronomer Royal to the Emperor, Albert Felicitas, Supreme Ruler of the Teutonic Empire.

Mercia was acknowledged by all to be as beautiful as she was talented; and the fame of her learning and genius was known throughout the Empire.

She was now thirty years of age, being still in the first bloom of womanhood; for woman was not fully developed until she attained the age of twenty-five, as the term of human life was augmented.

Man commonly reached his anticipated century of years; and it was no extraordinary occurrence to see a hoary-haired veteran of one hundred and twenty-five years surrounded by five or six generations of descendants who had assembled to do him honour on his birthday.

In former times Mercia would have been considered too tall for the ideal of womanly beauty, for she was five feet, ten inches, in height. Indeed, many women attained six feet in these days, but as they were perfectly proportioned, and graceful in movement, their great height gave no idea of awkwardness. Mercia's form was perfectly moulded, her limbs reminding the beholder of some chaste sculpture of the ancient Greeks, for her flowing robes partially disclosed their contour. Beneath the close-fitting sleeves of her tunic might be seen the fully developed muscles of her arms, which were exquisitely shaped; the firm wrist was small and round, the fore arm tapering upwards until the well-developed muscle of the upper arm was reached. This was not unduly prominent, but was softened and rounded beneath the clear skin, which, creamy white on the inner side, disclosed a faint pink shade on the outer, denoting the presence of perfect health. Her hands were moderately small, but perfect in shape ; the fingers were long and tapered, with deep, filbert-shaped nails ; indicating the intellectual cast of mind. The palm was tinged with a shell pink, while the back was of transparent, pearly whiteness, and fine as softest satin.

She was not brilliantly fair in complexion, but her skin was beautifully clear ; and the soft roses that tinted her oval cheeks paled, or deepened with her varying emotions.

Her beautiful starlike eyes were of an indefinable shade, being neither deep blue, nor brown decidedly. In the sunlight they beamed with a tint borrowed from the deep azure of the heavens just before sunset, in the shade they appeared a lovely, unfathomable brown.

Her nut-brown hair was long, fine, and silky, showing the mental temperament by its delicate texture. The head was fairly large, but well-shaped. The forehead, the seat of intellect, was high, broad, and full. Her eyebrows were well-arched, and curved in fair proportion ; but the space between the eyes was great, indicating very considerable development of the perceptive faculties.

It needed no brain-specialist to discover at the first glance that Mercia was born to her profession, for her powers of observation and reflection were mapped upon her brow.

Her long brown hair was arranged in glossy coils at the back of the head, in ancient classic style, showing its perfect contour ; while the curls near the forehead fluttering like flossy silk, and shimmering in the sun with a golden tint, softened the height of her broad and lofty brow.

Her breadth of chest indicated also that the physical part of her training had reached the fullest perfection. The open collar of her tunic partially disclosed her neck, Juno-shaped, and fine as cream-white satin.

In working hours she dressed in tunic, and trousers, made of dark, fine cloth, while her evening, or reception toilette was composed of flowing robes of bright, soft silk, which hung in graceful folds from her shapely bust, and down her well-formed limbs.

In her was seen personified modesty itself —not that of mere ignorance and shyness— but the modesty born of nobility of mind, wisdom, and purity.

Mercia was devoted to her profession; and so great was her enthusiasm that for fully six months in each year she made her observations of the heavens all night long, snatching only an hour or two in the daytime for sleep.

She had discovered with the aid of the powerful instrument that Geometrus, her chief assistant astronomer had invented, the existence of a number of new planets which revolved around one of the principal suns, hitherto unknown. The largest of these planets she named MERCIA, after herself; to its sun she gave the title of GEOMETRUS, in honour of the man she secretly loved, but dared not own it, not even to herself.

It was a law, or rather, a regulation which was strictly enforced that no Astronomer to the Emperor might marry. When a candidate for the post, which was deemed as honourable as that of prime minister, was successful, he was aware of the conditions his acceptance entailed. He was required to take a solemn oath to give up all thought of love, or matrimony, and devote the whole of his time, thought, and talent to the fulfilment of his duties, and the furtherance of the science of Astronomy, generally.

Astronomy, and Meteorology were considered by the nation such important branches of natural science, requiring in their pursuit so much self-denial that it was deemed an absolute necessity that whoever filled this important post should not be trammelled by the entanglements of love, nor ties of wedlock. For it was considered the uxoriousness of an affectionate husband, or wife, would while away the hours which otherwise would have been devoted to his, or her duties, these entailing long and severe rounds of night watchings.

It is true Mercia possessed the power to give up her post and marry; but to break the solemn oath she had given her Sovereign and country, to her pure and honourable mind appeared monstrous. Besides, such a course would have been attended with serious consequences, for to a certainty almost, Geometrus would be requested to resign his position, and thus both would lose, not only lucrative and honourable appointments, but employment which each enthusiastically loved for its own sake.

Geometrus was a tall, well-formed man of about thirty-five years; he stood in his soft leather shoes, which were formed exactly to the shape of the foot, at least six feet, two inches.

His complexion was somewhat similar to that of Mercia, for his hair and whiskers were of a bright brown; his eyes were dark and deep set: his nose was large and straight, but that was the prevailing characteristic of this time; for the nose being indicative of character, developed greatly, keeping pace with the growth of brain-power of which it is the sign, and outward index.

The mouth was firm, the lips being compressed, while the chin was prominent and broad.

In his face the brain specialist could easily

read his character, and judge correctly his special turn of mind.

Although he possessed, to some extent, the same powers of observation, reflection, and calculation as Mercia, still, his most prominent faculty was mechanics. In consequence of the excellent training he had received at the public schools of Astronomy, the bent of his genius was turned in this direction.

For this reason he made an admirable assistant to the Chief Astronomer, in so much, that he was always constructing wonderful instruments set with peculiarly formed lenses of his own invention, by means of which Mercia prosecuted with greater success her astronomical observations.

In truth, the two were made for each other; not only as co-workers, but also in disposition; for where there was a tendency towards an excess of fiery energy on the one side, it was met with the calm serenity of strict discipline on the other.

Mercia was of calm and even temperament, being wonderfully patient and enduring: the sweetness of her disposition was seldom

ruffled, even under the most trying circumstances. Although mild in manner, and in
speech, nevertheless she was by no means
apathetic or easy going, for her life was one
constant round of industry.

This rare combination of calmness and
energy had been transmitted to her by her
mother, a lady of great learning and talent,
who filled the appointment of Chief Inspector
of Public Schools under Government.

This lady realising fully the immense responsibility she was about to undertake when
becoming a mother, took all the precautions,
both physical and mental, to ensure having
for her offspring as perfect a human being as
was possible to obtain.

The effect of this *régime* on the part of
the mother, benefited herself equally as her
offspring; for when the hour of accouchement
arrived the pains of child-birth were so light,
and every muscle and organ of her body in
such perfect condition, that in the space of a
week she was fully restored and able to re-
sume her social, household, or professional
duties, as if nothing had happened.

There was no suckling of infants in these

days, except by the very lowest orders ; women having by degrees lost that property for some considerable time. As far back as the close of the nineteenth century this power had commenced to fail them.

Either through weakness engendered by much child-bearing, or the demands of society upon the time of the women belonging to the upper and middle classes, the habit of artificial suckling was resorted to, and eventually adopted by all classes about that period, with the result that in course of time Nature altogether refused to give any supply ; for she ever accommodates herself to the conditions under which she is placed.

Thus it came to pass that the mother was equally free as the father in the matter of nursing, if she elected so to be ; all the same, the child was still most carefully and skilfully tended.

The post of nurse was only filled by fully-trained, certificated women, who thoroughly understood the management of children, and who were competent to take them through any sickness without a doctor's assistance.

By this time the English language had

gained considerably by the introduction of words from all nations, who on their side returned the compliment by making it a speciality in their public schools, for English was the commercial language of the whole world.

But it became more than a commercial language to the Germans, for they dropping their own tongue with its uncouth gutturals, adopted the English, which was essentially their own, cultivated and enlarged, and made more musical.

Moreover another change was effected.

The ancient and primitive style was reverted to in the matter of the personal pronoun ; for the substitution of the plural 'you' for its singular 'thou' was considered ungrammatical, and therefore its use was deemed improper to continue.

This departure was imitated by the French who had been the original authors of the anomaly in the early centuries. However, among the lower orders, and in the fireside parlance the plural number was frequently retained.

At this period the Emperor Albert Feli-

citas reigned most peacefully over the Teutonic
Empire.  He possessed a palace in each capital, dividing his time among his various kingdoms with strict impartiality: not that it
mattered much where he resided, as the
means of locomotion had arrived at such perfection that a few hours' journey sufficed to
bring him to any part of his European Empire.

He wintered in Berlin in order to take
advantage of the fine frosts, and enjoy the
exercise of sleighing.  He summered in romantic Norway and Sweden ; utilising the
early spring months in travelling through his
Eastern and African Empires alternately, and
spent the beautiful autumn in England.

In his European dominions each country
retained its House of Parliament, which
possessed powers to make laws dealing with
domestic politics only ; these being afterwards sanctioned by the Emperor and his
Cabinet.  This was formed of four ministers
of each nationality, who were elected by
their country every seven years.

But a cloud was hanging over the fair
horizon of this happy Empire ; a deep dispute
had been growing for upwards of a century

between India and her rulers, formerly the British, but now the Teutonic Empire.

Western civilisation, or rather Western ideas, and education had brought the natives of the Eastern Empire to such a degree of culture and enlightenment that the subjugated ones realised that they had become the equal of their masters long before the dawn of the twenty-first century.

In point of fact, the close of the nineteenth century saw India supplied, not only with elementary schools, but ' High Schools,' and colleges of the first order, where the subjects taught met every want. They consisted of civil engineering, mathematics, experimental physics, mining, metallurgy, chemistry, architecture, forestry, farming, veterinary surgery, &c. In the College of Science, Poona, at this period all the foregoing subjects were taken. There was a farm of 150 acres in connection with this college which had been transferred by Government to the Agricultural Department; there were also a veterinary hospital where lectures were delivered; mechanical, physical and chemical laboratories, workshops, and foundries. A more complete arrangement for the training of young India could not have been devised. Here students of various nationalities, but chiefly Hindoos, studied and worked with the greatest enthusiasm.

Thus for a considerable period the natives had been availing themselves of the means of education afforded them so benevolently by the English Government, whose motto was ' Educate your subjects and they will better obey you ; ' whereas it should have been— ' Educate your servants and you make them your equals ; ' for knowledge gives power, or to define it more accurately in this case, knowledge gave insight, and discovered to its votaries the glories and delights of an enlightened liberty.

Notwithstanding the hindrances caused by religious superstitions they made excellent progress ; gradually emerging from the shackles of their ancient beliefs which acted as chains to keep them in the slavery of ignorance, they eventually became almost the equal of their rulers in manufactures, art, science, and literature.

Under these conditions they had become

a powerful people, and consequently were greatly dissatisfied with their position of dependence.

There had long been a growing feeling of dislike to the government of their country being consigned to the charge of a mere representative of the Teutonic Empire.

They considered that the time had arrived that such a vast and important Empire as theirs should be ruled by one supreme monarch, whose Court would suitably represent their country's wealth, power, and intelligence.

Once in the enjoyment of a Monarchical Government, tempered by the restrictions of a Constitutional, they felt they would be no longer handicapped as they had hitherto found themselves, for native gentlemen who had benefited their country to a marked degree, as well as men of acknowledged ability and genius, had, with rare exceptions, no titled honours conferred upon them as tokens of recognition of their worth. This omission they assigned to the jealousy of their rulers, coupled with their overweening opinion of Western superiority.

Thus to this very sensitive people it became a crying calamity that they had no Court of their own wherein they could create dukes, lords, and baronets *ad lib.* and set up a nobility and monarchy on their own account; on the same lines of government favoured by their Teutonic rulers.

Although India was universal in its desire for 'Home Government,' nevertheless, there were two great political parties in the country; one was conservative and desired a Monarchical, the other preferred a democratic or Republican form of government.

Of course the Press was the expression of these opinions, which the English and Germans eagerly perused, so that whenever a petition arrived at the Teutonic Court praying for freedom these opposing opinions were brought forward as an excuse for refusing their request.

'Why ask for powers of self-government' they retorted, 'when you are unable to agree upon what form it shall take? You are happier and better as you are for you know not how to govern yourselves; you are our children; we have educated you, and brought you up, as it were ; why desire to leave the parental control when it is only exercised for your good ? '

But the oppressed ones did not see it : they felt that they were only step-children, who were kept out of the benefits accorded the offspring of their rulers ; for all posts of honour and handsome remuneration had long been taken up by the overflowings of aristocratic Germanic and English families.

Even when in positions where natives were permitted the privilege of filling alongside the Englishman, as far back as the nineteenth century and upwards, natives were not remunerated with anything approaching the same rate of income as their more favoured colleagues ; although performing identical duties in the hospitals.

A reliable historian of the nineteenth century in treating this subject says :—' One serious obstacle in the way of increasing the supply of medical men, (natives) seems to me the unfair and invidious difference made in the remuneration of native as compared with English professional men employed in our service, and the same it may be added, applies to legal, and other departments of the State. Take Delhi, for example, where the civil surgeon, a military man, is paid 1,150 rupees per month, whilst his two native assistants receive only 150 each.  In Lahore the English civil surgeon gets 1,050 rupees, the native assistants 150 each.  Indeed, throughout India the proportion is everywhere as seven or eight for the English, to one for the native official.'

Is it to be wondered at that the dissatisfaction felt at the 'plums' being everywhere reserved for the British should begin to find utterance in the native Press, and in the National Congress?

So far as the medical department is concerned it cannot possibly be urged, as it is in the legal administration, that the moral qualities which are requisite demand a greatly increased scale of remuneration for the Englishman.  If the services of an English civil surgeon be worth 1,380*l.* per annum, surely those of his chief assistants, if they be of any value whatever, must be rated low at 180*l.*, no matter to what nationality they belong.

This does not apply, however, to the medical colleges and schools. For example, at the Campbell Medical School and Hospital, Calcutta, the superintendent, and English surgeon-major receive 550 rupees per month; and there are eight professors and demonstrators, *all natives*, most of whom get from 300 to 350 rupees, and a number of native assistants who receive 100 to 150 rupees.

'Can anything prove more conclusively that it is not the incapacity of the natives, but favouritism of the dominant race which awards disproportionately high salaries to the English officials?'

'Similar inequalities existed in most of the departments of the State, which were of vital importance to the political relations of the governors and the governed.'

Such were the outspoken sentiments of an Englishman whose high attainments and wide experience of Indian administration made his utterances worthy of the deepest consideration.

Side by side with Western culture grew the desire to imitate the Western system of home government. The initiatory movement in this direction took the form of an infant 'National Congress' which had its birth in the year of grace 1885, at Bombay, 'where seventy-two native gentlemen from all parts of India met together.' There were representatives from Karachi, Surat, Poona, Calcutta, Agra, Benares, Lucknow, Lahore, Allahabad, Ahmedabad, Bombay, Madras, Tanjore, and several other important places in India. Thus was constituted the nucleus of a greater and more important organisation, which ultimately developed with the growth of Western culture, for every educated Hindoo was as well acquainted with the social and political history of Great Britain and Ireland as any Englishman could possibly be. At this first Congress 'they spent three days in the discussion of questions affecting the interests of the native community, and in passing resolutions thereon.' The first resolution, which was supported by gentlemen of unquestioned standing, asked for a fulfilment of the ' promised inquiry' into the 'working of Indian administration, and suggested the appointment of a Royal Commission, the people of India being adequately represented thereon, and evidence taken both in India and England.'

'An expansion of the supreme and local legislative councils by the admission of a considerable number of elected members,' was another reform which was considered essential.

'Indirectly,' said the first report, 'this Conference will form the germ of a native parliament, and if properly conducted will constitute in a few years an unanswerable reply to the assertion that India is still wholly unfit for any form of representative institutions.'

The answer to these aspirations and desires on the part of the educated natives given by the governing classes in India practically were—'That the only government possible for India both in the interest of the British as well as of the natives, and as a protection against Russia, is a despotism.'

'That any concessions to native opinion will interfere with that despotism.'

'That the authority and domination of the officials must not be interfered with.'

'That if such concessions are made they

will only serve as an opening for further demands, the object being ultimately to overthrow the Government, and that the leading natives have that end in view.'

The prophets were correct : one hundred years later saw India with a fully fledged Parliament, enacting laws for her own government and finishing by demanding full control of Imperial politics, till finally the control of the conqueror, however mild, was sought to be banished completely.

There were those who were foolish enough to hint at extinguishing the Viceroy and all his court by means of electric lightning, but that course would have been idiotic in the extreme, for their rulers in turn could have annihilated the whole nation by the same process, so that to endeavour to settle the question by main force was simply impossible. Their grievance had by this time attained such magnitude that an immense requisition signed by millions of the inhabitants, or rather the natives, of India, was sent to the WORLD'S TRIBUNAL for consideration.

What a tumult this action put the whole world into! Thousands of books and pam-

phlets were issued on the subject in every
country. Throughout the globe newspapers
and monthly journals eagerly discussed the
question in their columns, and took sides
according to their trade or political relation-
ships with the countries in dispute, for self
ever predominates in the decisions of nations
as in those of individuals.

Notwithstanding all this literary energy
the 'Supreme Law of Nations' took its course.
Delegates from every Government were summoned to appear on May 1 in the year 2002 to
consider the secession of the Indian, from the
control of the Teutonic Empire, and all the
world wondered how it would end.

In due course a sub-committee was formed
from the delegates with powers to choose the
place in which the WORLD'S TRIBUNAL should
be held. It was finally decided that Paris
should be thus exalted, for this charming city
still held its own in the representation of the
science and art of the world.

The Chamber of Deputies for this unparalleled occasion was newly-decorated with
the greatest lavishness. Exquisitely upholstered chairs, resembling thrones in their

sumptuousness were provided for the occasion. The walls of the chief chamber in which the Court was to be held were beautifully decorated and made to appear like fine ivory, set in square slabs edged with gold: on each of the squares paintings of exquisite workmanship relieved the coldness of the pure cream-coloured ivory ground, while silken draperies skilfully embroidered with gold, in richest designs hung in graceful folds from windows and doorways. On the wall immediately behind the President's chair were suspended valuable paintings, the frames of which were composed of solid gold, whose corners were set with gems of great value.

Although much was done to please the eye in this temple of luxury, nevertheless, there was naught provided to tempt the palate.

The imagination of the ministers might revel in richest surroundings, but only the plainest fare was provided in the anterooms for their entertainment.

With these regulations, we may be sure, that the matter under consideration was not drawn out unduly, for who would remain in

a place where the pleasures of the table were
so scantily considered ?   No time being lost
in gastronomical or bibulous gratifications the
delegates were enabled to bestow assiduous
attention upon their duties, and listened carefully to the charges brought by the Easterners
against their governors.

They denounced emphatically the system
of vice-government which was rife with
abuses, and explained that from the very
commencement they regarded this foreign
intrusion as a degradation to their nation.
They pointed out that they were an ancient
people, possessing all the prestige of ages of
civilisation, who could not forget the glories
of bygone centuries ; for thousands of years
they had been governed by their own rulers,
in true Eastern magnificence ; at a period so
remote that their present rulers were then
mere barbarians, unknown to the civilised
world.  With such a past as theirs ; their
country possessing such classic associations.
standing proofs of which they had everywhere :
in the perfect architecture ; in their ancient
literature, all of which reminded them of
their former prestige and splendour.  The

time had arrived that they could no longer ignore the duty that lay before them, namely, to demand the restoration of their natural rights which had been filched away from them by fraud and deceit without their consent or desire. 'Yes!' continued the speaker, ' every inch of our territory has been surveyed and measured by the foreign intruder, and the products of our labour taxed heavily to uphold in luxury the children of the invader.'

It was the chief minister, Sir John Punjaub a leading Hindoo, who made this daring speech. He was a man advanced in years and full of learning, with ever so many letters after his name, indicating his membership of various scientific societies in England, Germany and India.

His countrymen adored him, for he had expended his vast wealth for their betterment, by the establishment of various philanthropic and educational institutions: but they loved him chiefest of all for his active enthusiasm in the promotion of their country's political welfare, and his kindly and ready sympathy in private life.

It was said of him that never in his life had he turned away from a tale of woe: ' Better,' he would say, ' give ten times to the unworthy, than once turn a deaf ear to the needy.'

The struggling youth who found the world too much for him in his first start in life would take heart of hope and whisper to himself—' I will go to Sir John, he will tell me what to do, and how I am to gain my goal: he sends no one away, he gives comfort and information; and if need be, funds to the honest worker who seeks his aid.'

Thus like the god of day, this dear old man imparted life and joy, and blessings wherever his influence reached, and the people in return reverenced and loved him greatly.

In the Eastern St. Stephen's he held the position of Prime Minister, and as a matter of course, upon him devolved the duty of stating the case of the Indian Empire before the WORLD'S TRIBUNAL.

He spoke in English of the purest diction. and pronunciation as perfect as that of a polished Englishman ; his great experience as a politician, his gift of eloquence and his profound wisdom, all combined to make him a unique interpreter of the feeling of India at this vitally important crisis.

The delegates listened in wrapt attention to every argument brought forward, giving assiduous attention to their duties throughout, and making notes of every point of any importance, on either side, all being done without the smallest loss of time. The result of such industry was that in fourteen days the whole of the evidence was gone through, after which the members of the Tribunal made their speeches, expressing their opinions upon the various points of the case in a clear and succinct manner.

This refraining from flowery oratory proved a capital saver of time, and brought the matter to a close much earlier than if all had disported themselves in high-flown rhetoric, or windy word-making.

By this time the expression of language had attained such perfection ; or rather, the gift of eloquence had become so general that almost everybody was able to express himself in well-chosen language with little or no preparation.

The result of this tongue-culture was a disfavour towards unnecessarily drawn out speeches. Indeed, the rule adopted mostly by legislative and other assemblies was timed speeches, generally from thirty to sixty minutes' duration ; but very rarely was this latter period taken except in cases of extraordinary importance.

It would astonish a nineteenth-century parliamentarian if he could have heard a thirty minutes' speech at this time. Every sentence uttered expressed a thought ; not a superfluous word was used throughout ; yet every idea was enunciated fully and perfectly, for it was concentrated thought projected in concentrated language.

For several previous generations this power of *précis* had been put in general practice. Both parents and teachers making it a point to impress upon children the vulgarity of verbosity ; both in writing and speaking an artistic method was inculcated that expressed every shade of thought in the least possible number of words.

Each day's proceedings at the World's Tribunal was known in every country upon the same day. In a couple of hours from the close of the chamber, the speeches appeared word for word, in the leading newspapers of every country, including the most distant parts of Africa.

Although eagerly perused by all, the contents were exceptionally interesting to India. Millions of dark eyes daily scanned the pages that brought them hope and fear alternately.

At length the day arrived upon which the decision was to be formally announced—it was the twenty-eighth from the commencement. Alas, the bright hopes of this gentle people were cruelly blasted, for the verdict of the Great Tribunal was against them.

At first overwhelmed with disappointment they were perfectly paralysed. A deep, dead silence reigned amidst that vast concourse of people while it was being read out to them ; for both high and low had assembled in immense crowds in some open space of each great city of India. This was followed by a sudden and furious anger that burst from the heart of the multitude and found vent in the loud cries of—' A trial by combat!  A trial by combat!'

The same day the Indian Press declared that the decision was unjust to a degree, nay, iniquitous; and the people of India should refuse to accept it.  Immediately America took up the strain and declared she had never approved of it, but having been in the minority when put to the vote their opinion had gone for nothing.

Then Russia had another word to say in the matter, and encouraged America, until eventually it was conceded that India should be accorded the benefit of the final test, and the great question decided by personal prowess.

To this arrangement the Teutonic Empire made no objection, for the natural confidence and conceit of the English caused them to regard with disdain an engagement where physical strength gave the victory.

Thus the most primitive method of settling a dispute was resorted to, when the verdict of experienced politicians failed.  Muscle-power was to prevail over mental even with the highly cultured people of this advanced period. The fact was, that however well-intentioned a conclave of politicians at the outset might be, there are so many influences at work, and so many international interests to consider, that to mete out justice with a Solomon-like impartiality proved more 'than human nature was capable of.

# CHAPTER II

## THE BATTLE

Now, as stated previously, the method of combat was entirely different from any practised in previous times, for the antagonist's life was not sought in any case, but disablement only. Victory was secured by rendering useless the right arm of the foe by giving it a blow with a short lance, or instrument electrically charged.

The peculiarity of this weapon was that it did not give an electric shock sufficient to kill a man, its effect being merely to paralyse the part it touched, and as the rule was to strike only at the right arm, no greater injury than the paralysis of that limb could take place.

Occasionally it happened that the arm was permanently paralysed; but mostly, only temporarily disabled, for clever electro physicians could commonly restore the limb by cunning administration of counter shocks which occasionally required several weeks, and even months, to effect a thorough cure.

Quack doctors had an evil time of it in these days; if any one took upon himself to publicly prescribe, or vend medicines without having obtained a proper diploma, he was arraigned and condemned to hard labour for a term of years. The employment he was put to usually consisted of the construction of public works, or something strictly useful, and sufficiently profitable to cover the expenses of his detention.

This too, was the reign of the specialist. In every trade, or profession such perfect knowledge was requisite that it was customary to take up but one branch and adhere to it solely.

For instance, a person with a nervous complaint would not dream of consulting a surgeon; the bone-setter never interfered with the fever patient; nor the aurist with the oculist; the child-doctor and accoucheuse kept strictly to her own department, except in rural districts, where there would not have been sufficient employment for each branch of medicine to be represented.

The solicitor never appeared in a police case; for another branch of the profession called ' petty pleaders,' conducted these, the study of which possessed its own separate course, and examinations. The food-chemist's diploma was not identical with that of the ordinary pharmaceutical chemist ; indeed, all the various branches of chemistry of which there was a great number, were separately chosen and studied with one definite end in view, everyone keeping to one thing, and doing that perfectly.

The country in which the contest should take place was decided by lot. The question was—India or England. And the lot fell on England. But it was indeed a difficult matter to discover a place sufficiently great in this thickly populated country which would be suitable for this immense tournament. Eventually, a space of sufficient area was fixed upon, which consisted of a number of fields of sweet-smelling flowers that were being culti-vated for the manufacture of perfumes ; for the wealthy still affected the natural perfume of distilled flowers, to the manufactured odours of the perfume-chemist.

These meadows formed a space of about two hundred acres, and being only a hundred miles from the metropolis proved most convenient for the purpose.

For several weeks previous to the day a large number of carpenters and upholsterers were busily engaged making the necessary preparations.

Tiers of seats to accommodate some thousands of persons were reared all round the field of combat, covered with crimson and gold cloth; while overhead were awnings of glittering silk composed of the finest drawn threads of glass, which shone brilliantly in the summer's sun. Indeed, robes of silk formed of this material were common enough, for the cocoon of the silkworm was insufficient to meet the demand for this favourite fabric.

But the throne, or seat of the Sovereign outshone all in magnificence. It was formed of beautifully carved coromandel wood, the natural markings of which presented the appearance of myriads of heads in countless variety of form. Therein could be seen the human face in every style of shape and expression; together with the heads of animals of every description.

This beautifully marked wood was relieved by inlayings of ivory, edged with gold.

The awning overhead which protected the monarch and his suite from the heat of the noon-day sun, or summer's shower, was also made of glass silk, the colours of which were artfully blended to represent the brilliant hues of the rainbow.

The daïs arranged for the accommodation of the umpires was also handsomely decorated : and when the field was filled with the richly-dressed knights of the silver lance, mounted on graceful steeds of surpassing elegance of form, it looked, indeed, like fairyland itself.

And now, behold, the day and hour have arrived for the great tournament, which has to decide the fate of the two contending Empires. Five hundred mounted, and an equal number of unmounted warriors on either side take their allotted positions, each armed with what appears to be a glittering silver lance, but is in reality an electrically-charged weapon whose only mission is to paralyse one particular limb of the adversary.

Dressed in crimson tunic, and steel-grey breeches, which displayed the well-formed proportions of the lower limbs, the lines of English combatants presented a most imposing appearance. Five hundred horsemen brilliantly attired, with silver helmets glittering in the sunshine, and mounted on well-trained steeds, awaited the signal to commence, while the same number of athletes on foot stood with eager looks in perfect readiness also.

The Indian athletes formed also a glittering galaxy of imposing splendour. Attired throughout in white and gold, their dark complexions set off by cream and gold helmets which shone bravely in the sunshine, they looked, indeed worthy antagonists for the bold and hardy Northerner. With lances drawn the combatants at the given signal now rush towards each other. Every man singles out his adversary, when a masterly piece of parrying takes place. With great skill and display of well-trained muscle-power the Eastern parries the Northern's stroke, which is unlike all hitherto known, it being allowable only on the right arm. If in the heat of battle an athlete should inadvertently hit his adversary in a vital part, and thereby cause his death, the unlucky contestant must himself pay a heavy money penalty to the family of the slaughtered man : this rule acted most beneficially, and formed on the whole a very safe life-insurance for each combatant.

The richly decorated galleries surrounding the scene of action are now filled with the *élite* of the whole world. Emperors, kings, czars, princes, and potentates of high position accompanied by their ladies beautifully attired make a *tout ensemble* that once beheld could never be forgotten.

Such a variety too, of costume as was never before seen grouped together, dazzled the beholder; for the Eastern style differed from the West as greatly at this time as in any previous period, but in a contrary way. During the lapse of many generations the Eastern had been gradually adopting the Parisian or Western mode of dress ; and the Western the flowing Eastern robes, until by this time the two modes were reversed ; or.

at least as much as our northerly climate would admit.

Thus it came to pass that a fair-haired English maiden would be attired in a flowing yellow silk robe, confined at the waist by a golden girdle, and at her side her mother stood draped in rich velvet that hung in graceful, flowing ripples from her shoulders; while the native of Turkey rejoiced in a tight-fitting bodice, with skirt beflounced and be-frilled in nineteenth-century Western style.

By this time the emancipation of Turkish women from their conventional imprisonment had taken place to their intense satisfaction. It was a long and hard battle this struggle for independence, and natural freedom, and was only gained eventually through the inter-vention of the chief women of the Teutonic Empire.

These were composed of lady members of Parliament together with the wives of the peers and nobles who in one great body went to the various potentates who had sliced up the country amongst them, to beseech them to advocate personal liberty to the female sex, in whatever degree or position in society they moved, and further exhorted them to use their influence with the people generally, to bring about this necessary reformation.

So the French, Russian, and Teutonic Empires graciously complied with the request of the fair delegates, and what is more, kept their royal promise to the best of their ability.

This was accomplished in part by the issuing of edicts to the people, who were first set the good example by the nobles whose interest it was to co-operate with their conquerors, or rulers : thus by degrees the women of the Teutonic race accomplished the emancipation of their sex in the lazy and luxurious East.

Never before was seen such a dazzling pageant as that viewed from the flying-machines which hung suspended in the air immediately above the scene of action. Seated in these aërial carriages their occupants could not fail to enjoy themselves, for they possessed the advantage of freedom to eat, drink and be merry, while they watched the fortunes of war as they developed in the field below without being hampered by conventionalities, or inconvenient onlookers.

At one moment they would see the Englishman parry the stroke of the Indian who was making a furious attack on his adversary. The Indian was indeed, struggling for dear liberty, and under this inspiration his naturally calm and placid countenance, whose expression betokened his gentle disposition, was fired with an enthusiasm that only a mighty occasion could call forth.

Ages of submission had given him a disposition to yield, for heredity is all-powerful, nevertheless, he fought against his nature, as it were, in order to obtain the benefits of that glorious liberty, of which the Briton himself boasted so constantly.

With this high resolve before his eyes, he set aside his natural instincts, and becoming another man, excelled himself, and fought the foeman bravely.

Thrust and parry; thrust and parry, went on for hours, until at last the sun was sinking in the horizon, and still the contest hung in even balance. Scores of men fell from the ranks on either side with one arm hanging helplessly at their side, while physicians with galvanic batteries stood in their tents outside the enclosure ready to render them needful service.

Time was up at six o'clock, and not too soon, for fighting had commenced at ten o'clock in the morning, and all were ready to drop with fatigue. Then the signal was given to cease, when the whole, or uninjured men were counted on each side; and to the intense disgust of the English who were ever proud of their prowess, and the great and exceeding joy of the unhappy Eastern the latter had won by just three men. Thus the patient and persevering Eastern worsted for once the bold and hardy Northerner. Then a ringing cheer burst forth from the thousand Indian athletes, and their friends; which was caught up by the people suspended above, filling the whole air with its shout of glad triumph. After all, Right had overcome Might in this great struggle, which finally settled the dispute of many generations.

Among the two thousand contestants only twelve casualties occurred; in other words, twelve men lost their lives in the encounter. Of these seven were Hindus; but they died in a glorious cause and their names were

handed down to posterity by the erection of
a splendid malachite column on which was
inscribed their names and a graceful tribute
of their countrymen's gratitude in verse.
This was composed by their beloved minister,
whose splendid appeal at the Great Tribunal
had failed to move the hearts of their judges ;
but the little verse, noble in its simplicity and
tender pathos, brought the unconscious tear
to the eyes, not only of the admiring Native,
but also to the Briton himself, who no longer
grudged the Eastern his well-deserved victory.

# CHAPTER III

'Of queenly mien, of loveliest form, and eyes
  Like gems set in translucent skies.
  And all the beauty of the Court was dimmed
  By fair Igerna : to Uther's eyes she seemed
  To stand a peerless pearl ; a diamond divine ;
  Beyond all price, and fitted most to shine
  In kingly coronet of the great on earth,
  A prizeful jewel of unbounded worth.
  . . . . All women she outvies
  In every gentle grace.  Her voice now thrilled
  With soft delight his ravished ears, and filled
  His listening soul with music's harmony,
  Sweet as the rippling water's melody.'

Idylls, Legends and Lyrics.

THE Royal Observatory was a stately building
of great height erected close to the old building in Greenwich Park, which latter was kept
as a show place, and used also as a lecture
hall for students of Astronomy.  The lower
apartments of the new building were occupied
by Mercia and her household, while the upper
rooms were devoted to the purposes of her
profession.  A suite of rooms on the left wing

were set apart as workshops for Geometrus, whose spare time was always taken up with planning or perfecting some wonderful astronomical instrument more powerful than the world had hitherto seen.

In a spacious apartment on the third floor which contained two powerful telescopes, constructed on principles of entirely modern invention, being capable of revealing the distant suns to an extent never before dreamt of, was Mercia surrounded by curious astroscopes, stellar-spectroscopes, and wonderfully constructed cameras, which delineated in an instant the starry heights, the glory of which has been the ambition of astronomers in all ages to fathom.

She was seated at her desk making some mathematical calculations of the celestial depths, and was so completely engrossed in her labours that the entrance of her fellow-worker, Geometrus, went unheeded. At length, coming to a close, she raised her head, when instantly a flush of pleasure brought the rose more vividly into her cheeks.

'Ah, Geometrus, is it thou?' she exclaimed, 'I have finished the measurement of thy namesake, the fixed star, and am happy at last. His system of planets are now all perfect before me : I must write a treatise on this new addition to science so that posterity may know what we have attained.'

'Why use the word " we," my mistress,' replied the young man, 'it is thou alone who hast done the work?'

'It is true that I have made the observations and calculations, Geometrus, but it was thy cunning which formed the instrument. Take thy due, my friend, and be not over modest; some base imitator may some day defraud thee of thine invention, unless thou wilt consent to acknowledge it openly.'

'I would that I might acknowledge openly the one deep thought of my heart,' he answered with a sigh as he turned to leave the apartment.

'Stay a little while, Geometrus, I would have some converse with thee. I am buried so deeply in my work that I know not how the world is wagging. What about the great dispute that is coming before the World's Tribunal? Is it a righteous cause this of the Eastern, thinkest thou?'

'Nay, mistress, that is not for me to settle: judge for thyself. India desires to regain her ancient freedom. The Government reins of the foreigner however lightly held, gall her. She does not deny having received great benefits from the invader, as great as the Romans conferred upon the early Britons: nevertheless, she would prefer a measure of mismanagement under a native ruler, than the most perfect arrangements from the stranger.'

'But it is folly in these enlightened times to imagine that India, once our rule were withdrawn, would revert to the old order of things. Ignorance and superstition, Eastern despotism and tyranny can never again find a home in that beautiful country,' remarked Mercia thoughtfully.

'Oh, we are all well aware of that: but it suits our purpose to make these assertions: we must invent a *raison d'être* when we take upon ourselves the government of a country that in no way belongs to us. It is *pro re natâ*—for a special business—that we aver they can't get along without us. We have edged in little by little until we have brought the whole Empire under our dominion. To give up India now, would be as tantalising to us, as it would be to the victorious soldier if asked to give up his loot; for in the good old times pillage was the perquisite of the warrior. America evidently sympathises with India in her desire for a monarchy. That country pretty well understands where the shoe pinches for she has gone through experiences.'

' I have read in books,' observed Mercia smiling, ' how American women made wealthy by their parents' success in trade, came hither to mate with titled men; for there was no nobility in their own country. I suppose possessing all the world could give save high rank they sought in the parent country for that which their own lacked.'

' They lacked not long,' returned Geometrus laughingly, ' for over fifty years they have been in the enjoyment of a monarchy and all its concomitant honours. The image and superscription of King Jonathan, the First, that adorns the almighty dollar impresses one painfully with their pinchbeck royalty.'

' We shall get used to it in time,' observed Mercia gently. ' A young republic cannot

make an old monarchy. After all, there was
a spice of modesty in Jonathan when he
elected a king, for he might have made him
an emperor while doing it.'

'It wasn't modesty at all—it was selfish
prudence; they wanted to follow the lines of
a constitutional monarchy and considered it
was the safest thing to call their Figure Head
a king.'

'If India obtains her desire I wonder
whom she will chose for Emperor. Doubtless
the people will want that dear old Prime
Minister of theirs; they could not have a
worthier monarch.'

'But he is old,' replied Geometrus quickly,
' and he is childless, what is to become of the
succession when he dies? There will arise
tumults and internal quarrels as to his successor: better choose a younger man, and one
likely to found a lasting royal line. Remember the fate of Germany. Had there been a
goodly half-dozen of sons to fall back upon
an English prince would never have had the
chance of their crown.'

'All's well that ends well, Geometrus.
Now is England invincible to the whole world:

in her position as a united Empire her power is paramount everywhere.'

No sooner had Mercia made this observation than she heard the sound of some unusual noise going on outside, and stepping to the window she saw several gentlemen assembled near the Observatory, among whom she discerned no other personage than the Emperor Felicitas himself.

' Here's a pretty surprise for thee, Mistress Mercia,' exclaimed Geometrus excitedly; ' none other than the Emperor !  It is not I he seeks, but thou, Mistress Mercia, I will then away.'

' Stay, Geometrus ! ' exclaimed Mercia quickly, ' I would prefer thy company when I receive the Emperor.  I will now retire and change my dress for a more suitable habit in which to receive so honourable a visitor.'

But before she could leave the room a messenger was at the door desiring an audience for his royal master.

Mercia silently bowed her assent ; and a moment later the monarch entered her studio. As he did so she rose from her seat at the large table, which was covered with charts and maps of the celestial regions, all of her own making, but the Emperor quickly stepping forward observed gallantly, 'Stay, lady, keep thy seat, for it is meet that monarchs should serve thee, who art so full of knowledge and wisdom.'

'Thou art my master,' she answered in a grave tone.

'Thy Sovereign, yet thy servant,' he replied with a deep bow.

'What is thy wish, Sire, wherefore am I honoured by this visit?'

'I would know, fair Mercia, the cause of this change of temperature, not only in my dominions, but from all accounts I hear it is general throughout the world. For three successive years an extreme cold has prevailed each season. I fain would learn the reason.'

'Some serious internal changes are taking place within the body of our sun. Great caverns, about one-fourth of the sun's diameter have discovered themselves in his centre. We are not the only planet-dwellers suffering from cold at this time, for a difference will be experienced throughout the whole of the solar system. But it is only a temporary inconvenience; from close observation I find that our sun is absorbing numerous meteoric bodies, of which there are billions wandering in interstellar space, that have been projected from the innumerable suns still called stars by the people, and for the sake of convenience the title is retained by physicists. I conclude therefore that there is no cause for alarm. Our sun has indeed sent out of himself great projectiles into space, but he is ever capturing wandering bodies that happen to come within his influence. In this way the hydrogen of the fixed stars is pressed into our sun's service and a constant heat sustained, which may last for thousands of years to come.'

'Of all the stars thou studiest nightly to such excellent purpose, thou art the brightest, Mercia. Thou art truly the wisest of women; and as fair as thou art far-seeing. Thy words give comfort to the world, and thy beauty brings thy Sovereign much delight.'

While Felicitas was uttering these pleasant gallantries, he was gradually edging his chair nearer and nearer to that of Mercia.

Mercia's countenance at once assumed a more serious expression; hastily glancing

towards that part of the room where Geometrus was seated she found he had slipped out
unobserved, doubtless with the intention of
leaving them quietly to their discussion on
the sun's condition.

'Truly, it is most kind of thee, Sire, to
show such appreciation; but I seek no
flatteries, or compliments—nay—I will have
none of them,' she answered with downcast
eyes.

'Why, what harm is there in speaking a
truth, Mercia?  I do affirm that thy beauty
only exceeds thy knowledge, or thy knowledge thy beauty, I know not which.'

'Be it so, then, Sire.  It is nothing to my
credit if I be beautiful; I had no part in the
making; and as to my knowledge, it is a
necessity to possess it, for it is my livelihood
—my very bread.'

'Ah, Mercia, why spoil those eyes more
beautiful than the brightest star in gazing
into unknown regions day and night; year
in, year out?  Thou knowest no enjoyment—
thou hast no pleasure of life, as other women;
thine existence is lonely—colourless.  Drink
of the draught of love as nature wills it, and

let the study of the stars stand over for a space.'

The voice of Felicitas as he uttered these words was low, but full of passion; but Mercia, owing to the confusion that covered her, did not notice the change of tone. The king's words had indeed evoked emotions in her breast that for years she had kept in strict abeyance: now, these throbbed and pulsated through her frame with such force that she became dumb, tongue-tied; at this inopportune moment a knock was heard at the door, and the Emperor himself touched the electric button, when the door opened of itself and gave admittance to another visitor.

It was only Geometrus who had returned for a part of an instrument he was making, which he had inadvertently left behind; his entrance, however, put a prompt stoppage to the Emperor's love making; and Mercia, hardly knowing what she was doing rose from her seat and turned to leave the apartment; observing her intention the Emperor concluded that it was time to withdraw.

'Farewell, mistress,' he said lightly, as he made her a bow, 'I will come again, ere long and learn of thee the sun's condition which is so necessary to be acquainted with.'

It was the fashion at this time to call a woman 'Mistress,' whether married or single. The abbreviation 'Mrs.' was discarded, as was also 'Madam' borrowed from the French, and the old English style resumed in their stead ; while 'Miss' was applied only to children. The married woman was distinguished from the unmarried by the possession of two sur-names,—her father's and husband's, while the single woman was known by her father's name only.

Mercia, in order to escape from observation quickly made her way into her most private apartment, and shutting herself safely within she sank upon the silken couch, and gave way to the tumult of feelings that over-whelmed her.

What did the Emperor mean by coun-selling her to relax in her duties and give way to the passion of love? she asked herself. Was he putting her probity to the test, merely to ascertain of what stuff she was made? or was it only a random shot on his part, made for mere amusement, but which had unwittingly touched her deepest feelings? Did he suspect her affection for Geometrus?— but that was impossible; not a living soul knew that she loved this man, not even Geometrus himself. Had Geometrus betrayed himself in any way? Was it possible that in some unguarded moment he had spoken of his passion for her to some friend who had afterwards betrayed him to the Emperor? No, that was impossible. Geometrus would not dare to speak of that which he was prohibited from even hinting at to herself. Had some person, envious of her position, invented some tale, and carried it to Felicitas with a view of bringing about her downfall? If so, who could it be? Was it Heinrich, the German, who longed for her post, and had he done this dishonourable thing to obtain it?

Then the thought crossed her mind of the possibility that the Emperor might have been saying something for himself, of which the bare idea brought the crimson to her cheeks: but this solution of the question she endeavoured promptly to dismiss, for Felicitas was already married, and to offer her, Mercia, an illicit love would be an unparalleled presumption, even from an Emperor.

'What can have put this abominable thought into my head?' she again asked herself. Then she rose from her seat and paced up and down her chamber with perturbed motions and flushed face.

She felt that the whole thing was mystifying to a degree. At length, after much cogitation she concluded to take no further notice of the matter, for it would be undignified to seek explanations either of Geometrus or the Emperor.

'Let me take up a position of inactivity,' she murmured to herself, 'I will await developments as they unfold, and shape my course accordingly.'

Did the Emperor dream of success in his endeavour to corrupt the faultless Mercia? It was, indeed, a bold step for him to take with one so high-minded, so self-controlled as she. But her very unattainability made her all the more desirable in his eyes: the more he dwelt on the futility of his wish the more violently his passion raged within him.

'I must have Mercia!' he exclaimed to

himself as nightly he lay awake dwelling on her beauty, her goodness, and her extraordinary abilities.

'She must be mine, I cannot live without her! I will go to her again—I will risk all, and tell her of my love. If need be, I will break down that barrier that divides us; I will not be baulked of Mercia. If she refuse to become mine secretly, I will wed her openly, and get rid of that flat-faced Russian woman whom my ministers talked me into marrying.'

Now Felicitas spoke wildly when he gave way to these thoughts, for it was impossible to put away the Empress, he having no adequate cause given him to justify such an attempt. Russia would indignantly resent such treatment of their Princess, and none of the foreign Powers would stand by him in his demand.

From nineteenth-century immorality covered by the thick cloak of religion, a change had gradually taken place for the better in matters matrimonial. In fact, a high standard of morality in all things had taken the place of religious superstitions; consequently, the teachings of common sense were adopted in the remodelling of divorce laws, which for ages had contained serious blemishes. This, in part, was owing to the absurd restrictions of the clergy of those times, the upper members of which body holding the position of chief legislators together with the peers of the realm.

These insisted on the indissolubility of the marriage tie, as far as ever it was possible to make it, quoting ancient Mosaical laws in support of their views, as if those old-time regulations which were probably suitable enough in their day for the primitive people for whom they were framed, should continue as a guide for all ages.

But long before Felicitas' time a great revolution had taken place in laws matrimonial, which benefited society very materially. These were now framed on more equitable principles, for the truest benevolence pervaded their spirit, the punishment of the guilty one being not the only object sought, as in nineteenth-century law, which forbade the divorce, if it was discovered the two were agreed for it, but rather the happiness of both. Marriage was now regarded as a serious civil contract which could not easily be violated, but relief from its yoke was allowed under certain conditions, without either party having been conjugally unfaithful. If a couple living a notoriously unhappy life, and finding they were totally unadapted for each other, finally agreed to separate, it was possible to get the marriage contract annulled, and the two set at liberty again.

The children of the marriage, if any, would be equally divided between them, or some amicable arrangement arrived at.

This severance did not relieve the husband of the responsibility of her maintenance, except in cases where the wife possessed sufficient means of her own to live upon, or in the event of her marrying again, when of course, all responsibility on his part ceased.

It may be imagined that the Divorce Courts were kept pretty lively by these innovations; it certainly had this effect for some little time; but gradually as education and the higher morality advanced the number of annulled marriages decreased.

As soon as the social plane for woman was raised she became more exacting in her requirements, preferring to remain single rather than mate with the morally weak, or otherwise unsuitable person.

To a man marriage was not the easy matter it had been to the nineteenth-century bachelor, when numbers of unemployed, or,—owing to their absurd training—hopelessly incompetent young women were to be had for the asking. But this was all changed now; a desirable wife had become as difficult to obtain as a desirable husband in previous generations; and when a man's suit proved successful, and he had gained the object of his choice, he usually behaved in such a way towards her as gave her considerable satisfaction.

On her side too, rested a responsibility which she realised to the utmost; and willingly yielded to the man she had elected the devotion of a high minded, unselfish affection.

Love, in its purest form was woman's ideal, for the heart as well as the intellect was culti-vated.

# CHAPTER IV

' Your wondrous, rare description, noble Earl,
Of beauteous Margaret hath astonished me.
Her virtues graced with external gifts,
Do breed love's settled passions in my heart ;
And like as rigour of tempestuous gusts
Provokes the mightiest hulk against the tide,
So am I driven, by breath of her renown
Either to suffer shipwreck, or arrive
Where I may have fruition of her love.'

*King Henry VI.,* sc. v.

WE left Mercia somewhat settled in her mind regarding the course she ought to take with the Emperor.

If Felicitas should chance not to make mention of the subject of love, which was a forbidden one to her, owing to her position, she made up her mind to forbear making inquiries concerning his motive for introducing it.

She waited and watched each day for his coming with a vague hope in her heart that he would look favourably upon Geometrus' love, in the event of his having knowledge of it. In any case, it could only be a suspicion, seeing it was as yet undeclared on his part.

Although she said nothing to Geometrus, nevertheless, he felt there was something in the air. Often he would look at her wistfully and try to probe her thoughts; for he saw most distinctly the preoccupation of her mind as she strove to make her usual mathematical calculations. Still he forbore questioning her, for the one subject he was desirous of discussing with her, was entirely forbidden. Only his eyes told of the love that filled his heart.

Reason reminded him that it was indeed a hopeless affection, for he felt assured that Mercia's mind was so bound up in her vocation that she could never be induced to abandon it in order to wed one who had so little to offer her in return. Moreover, he too, would be sent adrift as soon as the matter oozed out, for the same prohibition from marriage was placed upon him.

Numerous, indeed, were the plans he formed daily in his mind of what he would do for a competent livelihood in the event of his acceptance by Mercia. He knew it was useless to make her an offer unless he could see his way clear to maintain her, when to accept him she must abandon a highly lucrative and honourable position.

'But would she indeed make such a sacrifice for him?' he asked himself, 'Would it not be selfish on his part to prefer such a request? True—true; he would not—dare not make it. It was selfish, utterly selfish to dream of it for one moment. No, he would lock up his feelings; he would carefully keep his heart-secret; he would not ruin her life by asking her to share his comparatively humble position, supposing she was willing to listen to him.'

Thus did Geometrus torment himself with many doubts and fears. At one moment making bright plans for the future, wherein he saw himself distinguished before the world for his wonderful instruments, the like of which he knew had never been produced before, and probably would be at no time beaten. These had been planned and invented in the first instance for Mercia alone, yet for Mercia's sake they should be given to the world, so that he might become more worthy of her; a more honourable mate for the peer-less Mercia.

Ah, Love, Love, how much thou hast to answer for! How many human hearts hast thou set wildly beating for fame that would otherwise have remained in quiet seclusion? How many mighty minds hast thou set daily and nightly throbbing with pain by reason of thine unreasonable attraction? Thou seekest thine affinity where it is forbidden thee to enter, ever regardless of the restrictions and barriers invented by mankind for their pro-tection.

Thou only dost behold the object of thy search; invisible to thine eyes the barricades .of worldly conventions.

Quite alone, and unattended by any member of his suite, Felicitas set off to pay Mercia his promised visit; who on her side gladly gave him a pleasant welcome. In her heart she fondly hoped that the interpretation of his words would prove favourable to herself and Geometrus; and in some way yet to be discovered, the monarch might benefit them.

For could he not influence his ministers to

do away with this absurd marriage objection ? Yes, Felicitas had power to help them, if he could be induced to put it into operation. This was the one thing needful; the monarch's goodwill, and all would then be plain sailing.

Their marriage need not hinder their work ; they two could labour together, she thought, and side by side discharge conscientiously their allotted duties, to their country's satisfaction and their own perfect content.

It so happened that Geometrus on that day had business in the city, which detained him several hours, and as the Emperor was being driven in a carriage drawn by horses— for this was the custom of royalty, that it should be distinguished from the commonalty, who used electric force for cheapness as for swiftness—he saw Geometrus enter a machine warehouse, or shop, where electrical household machines were vended.

'Ah,' thought the Emperor, 'thou art there, my friend : pray make no hurry on my account; thou wast truly *de trop* on the last occasion I called on mine astronomer ; I could well have spared thy presence.'

Thus the Emperor felicitated himself upon

his good fortune, in being secured against a like interruption on this occasion. When arrived at his destination, which was not very soon, owing to the slowness of the journey—for the speed of the horse was not comparable with that of electric energy—the Emperor entered the Observatory with a firm resolution to make good use of the opportunity with which fortune had favoured him. Now, Mercia, with the same motive in her mind, received him very cordially, for she desired to make a favourable impression, with a view of obtaining his royal clemency in the matter of matrimony, albeit, it appeared on further reflection, but a bare possibility that she would at any time change her present condition.

'Ah, Mistress Mercia,' he exclaimed playfully, 'what cheerful looks thou dost carry to-day, methinks thy face betokens much content—hast thou taken my words to heart, fair lady, 'twas truly excellent advice?'

'Sire, thou saidst something concerning the sun—thou didst talk of coming to learn more of his condition, I believe,' answered Mercia evasively.

'True,' he replied with a laugh, 'I fain

would know more of the sun's late vagaries : but it would please me infinitely better to learn something of thyself, dost thou never feel lonely ? '

' Often enough, Sire ; the hours speed away at times very quickly when I am hard at work, but when it is time to rest then the feeling of solitude overwhelms me : I get appalled at the silence that surrounds me, and a melancholy seizes me so severely that I rise unable to cope with my duties.'

' Art thou then tired of this occupation ? It is indeed, too much for thee. Rest a while, sweet Mercia, and let the stars take care of themselves for a season.'

' Oh, that would spoil all my calculations ; the work of years would be as naught were I to stay my hand now. No, I will wait until my treatise on the stars is complete ; then I will take some little change for my health's sake.'

' Health, and Love, sweet Mercia, go hand in hand together. Let thine heart melt to its influence, and all will go well with thee. Thy melancholies will disappear ; thy solitude lightened ; for thou wilt have a new theory to analyse—a new and a better one.'

' Yes, thou canst love, dear Mercia, I know it ; for thine eyes were made for the conquest of man's heart, rather than star-gazing. Cease to disregard the designs of Nature when she formed thee, and yield thyself to the pleasure of love.'

Mercia essayed to answer him, but her tongue refused her utterance, so great was her confusion. She blushed violently, and at last stammered out—

' Sire, I know not what answer to give in this matter—I am yet unprepared,—perplexed with this reasoning of thine.'

' Hast thou not felt the want of companionship, dear Mercia? Here penned in this solitude only fit for a greybeard thou dost pine, yet knoweth not what it is ails thee. It is good to be loved, fair one, to realise how much thy womanhood means : hast thou never felt its joys—its pains ? '

' But my bond, Sire, I cannot break my bond, signed by my own hand, to forswear love and marriage : no one but thyself can relieve me of this obligation,' exclaimed Mercia excitedly.

' I heartily relieve thee, then, my good

Mercia. I care not for the bond one iota, if that be all that's in thy way. Keep thy post as thou likest thy work so well, and enjoy the delights of love at the same time,' replied the delighted monarch, who found it most difficult to conceal his fancied triumph.

Mercia uttered a low cry of joy, and in her gratitude threw herself at his feet, then taking his willing hand in hers, she pressed it to her lips in silence, for her heart was too full for speech.

When the matter had arrived thus far. the Emperor forgetting the caution and self-restraint he had been hitherto exercising, was no longer able to contain himself; stooping down towards the kneeling girl he caught her in his arms, and in a perfect frenzy of rapture commenced to shower hot kisses on her brow. her cheeks, her lips.

Mercia was so completely taken aback by this unexpected raid, that her brain fairly reeled for a moment; then recovering her senses she quickly wrenched herself out of his arms, and gazing on him with blanched face, she cried in a voice gasping with pain and indignation—

'What means the Emperor by this unheard of liberty? What have I done that I should be treated as a courtesan by my Sovereign?'

'A courtesan!' he repeated. 'Why Mercia, I would give thee a crown if I could! Thy queenly brow was truly made for one; and by the stars, thou shalt have it yet! Yes, Mercia thou shalt share my throne and rule me, my sweet, together with mine Empire.'

'Share thy throne and rule thine Empire! Surely, Sire, thou hast gone mad!'

'Yes, truly, I am mad—mad with love for thee, and thou knowest it, Mercia, else wouldst thou have kissed my hand in acknowledgment of it?'

'In acknowledgment of *thy* love!' she answered in strong indignant tones, 'it was not so—thy love never entered my thought.'

'Whose then?' questioned Felicitas shortly.

'Geometrus,' she acknowledged bravely. But the next moment she felt she had given away both herself and him.

'Geometrus!' he scoffingly repeated. 'And dost thou place that poltroon before me? Am I to be flouted for him?'

' His love is honourable, and thine is not ; therein lies the difference, my Sire,' she answered soothingly, with a view of bringing him to reason.

' But my love *shall be made* honourable, Mercia. I will get a divorce, and thou shalt fill the Empress's place—aye, and fill it far away better than she has ever done ! I hate her—curse her !' And he ground his teeth in rage at the thought of his wretched inability to accomplish what he was so loudly boasting of.

' But I cannot rob another woman of her husband : I would not defraud the meanest in thy realm, much less thine Empire's highest lady.'

' It is not robbery, Mercia, she doth not own my heart, and never did ! I was cozened into that marriage by my cousin Osbert—curse him—curse him for a meddling fool !'

' He, doubtless, did it for the best. The whole of thy Cabinet approved, so did the nation. It is a new thing for me to learn that our Emperor lives unhappily with his spouse —I cannot understand it.'

' I never felt the chains gall till now,

Mercia. A quiet indifference kept me content until thy beauty set my heart abeating with a new joy. I knew not love till mine eyes dwelt upon thy loveliness, and mine ears listened to the words that flowed from thy lips like a sweet, rippling fountain, whose waters gave forth a pure, clear, lifegiving stream. Yes, I have drunk therein, and am filled with new emotions—new joys—new hopes—new life!' He clasped his hands in an ecstasy of happiness, as at that supreme moment he gave rein to the powerful impulses that swayed him.

'Now is my beauty an evil thing, and a curse to me!' cried Mercia, at the moment bowing her head in deep dejection, and hiding her face in her hands.

'Would I had never been born, or that nature had shaped me uncomely, for then this misfortune could not have overtaken me! Two men desire me, and I may not have either. I must live in a world filled, like a garden with flowers—flowers and blossoms of love; yet I may not touch them; their fragrance is not for me; not one may I wear on my breast! Yet, they nod and beckon me to pluck them: they offer me the incense of their being, and would fain spend their full fragrance upon me; for their desire is to nestle on my bosom, and give me the joy of their beauty and love.'

She spoke as one entranced, who ignoring all listeners felt naught of the presence of another. For the moment her anguish was her only companion, which the presence of Felicitas could not restrain. It was the bursting wail of a heart kept long in subjection and unnatural restriction, which now claimed its rights. Thus did the longing for love bring sorrow to Mercia, such sorrow as she had never before tasted.

As Felicitas gazed upon the beautiful woman standing before him in an attitude of grief and despair, her head bowed down, her arms outstretched, showing the contour of her perfect form, he felt as one in a dream—a ravishing dream that inspired every sense with a deliciousness he had never before experienced.

On his enraptured ears her words fell like the music of a poem, for the full, rich, melodious *timbre* of her voice lent to them a peculiar charm: their pathos melted him; their sweetness enchained him.

Seized anew with the intoxication of his

passion he sank on his knees before her; his whole frame quivered with emotion, while the varying tones of his voice testified how greatly the torrent of his passion swept through his soul.

'Mercia, Mercia, give me thy love!' he cried impetuously; 'take me, my beloved, spurn me no longer, for without thee I am as one dead! As a world without sun, having no life, nor warmth, I shall go on my way darkened for ever. Take me into the sunshine of thy love; give me new life, dearest. Resuscitate and refresh me with the joy of thy beauty; and let us drink of the wine of love's pleasures for ever. Then shall we two learn how good it is to love; how sweet it is to be together; how delightful the blending of two souls made satisfied with their own companionship.'

As one in a dream Mercia listened to his passionate outpourings; she drank in his words as gratefully as the parched earth a summer's shower; but her mind was with Geometrus. In imagination she was with him, listening to the pent-up eloquence that his soft dark eyes daily expressed.

'It is Geometrus who speaks!' she murmured absently; 'Geometrus has opened his heart to me at last!'

'Geometrus!' shouted the Emperor, almost out of his head with rage and jealousy; 'it is *not* Geometrus—it is I, Felicitas—Felicitas thine Emperor who abjectly offers thee his love, and his crown, and sues thee, Mercia—his subject—his servant!'

Then Mercia, awakening from her love-dream began to realise her true position. For an instant she paused, and passed her hand across her brow, as if to recover her senses; then she said in a deliberate and dignified voice—

'Felicitas, the Emperor hath no crown to offer his subject, Mercia, for it sits already on the brow of his royal spouse; neither has he love to offer his servant, Mercia, for it is sworn to his Empress for ever. It is an insult to me, Mercia, thine offer of illicit love, and I refuse to longer remain in thy service.'

Upon hearing these words the heat of his temper suddenly cooled; he saw he had not only ruined his cause with the lady, but he

was bringing upon himself public dishonour ;
for the reason of the resignation of their gifted
and enthusiastic astronomer would be demanded by both ministers and nation alike.
As she turned to leave the apartment, for she
disdained having further converse with him,
he forcibly caught her by the dress, with a
view of detaining her.

'Stay, Mercia, stay, and listen to me! Listen
to one word more, I beseech thee. Thou
shalt, for indeed I will not let thee go!' He
shouted fiercely, for she was wrenching herself out of his grasp.

'Touch me not!' she exclaimed excitedly, 'or I will kill thee as thou standest!'
and from her girdle she took a small ebony
stick, electrically charged, which she wore as
a kind of life-preserver, in accordance with
the custom of ladies, who worked, or walked
out a good deal alone.

She had reached the door, and opened it,
when who should rush upon the scene but
Geometrus accompanied by the Emperor's
cousin, Prince Osbert, who had been seeking
him for some time past.

'Mercia insulted, and by the Emperor!

What is the meaning of this?' inquired Geometrus, at the same time facing Felicitas with eyes of fire.

'I am not insulting her,' coolly rejoined the Emperor, 'she has disobeyed my commands respecting some important astronomical information I required, and is endeavouring to shield her own shortcomings by getting into a rage: 'tis woman's way, but I'll have none of it.'

Then Mercia drawing herself up to her full height, exclaimed in indignant voice—'Liar, and traitor, I despise thee! Bid thine Empress come hither, I have somewhat to tell her. As for me, I shall never receive thee here again, thou woman-betrayer! Get some other to fill my place, for I shall quit it forthwith.'

Then she turned away with haughty mien and left the apartment.

'What's all the row?' inquired the Emperor's cousin, who affected vulgarity of speech when with his intimates.

'Explain this, Sire,' demanded Geometrus, who was bursting with surprise equally as indignation.

' Bah, it is naught—it is much ado about nothing,' replied the Emperor shrugging his shoulders.

' I do not believe it,' promptly answered Geometrus ; ' my mistress is too gentle, too self-restrained, and too honourable to make an unjust accusation against anyone ; least of all, her royal master.  This matter shall be looked into, Sire.  Though thou art an Emperor thy conduct shall be examined, and the light of the noonday sun thrown upon it; for it is meet that those filling high places be honourable men.'

' If Mistress Mercia sees fit to give up her post, thou Geometrus canst worthily fill it,' observed Felicitas in an insinuating manner, hoping to mollify him by offering to place him in a more exalted position.

' By all that's good, I take not my mistress's place because thou hast made it intolerable for her !  No, Sire, that shall not be. But certainly thou shalt answer for this day's work, I warn thee.'

' Thou hast no proof at all, fellow, that I have done aught amiss, save her lying tale : it is all a woman's hysterical nonsense, and I am sick of the pother made of it,' observed the Emperor, affecting great scorn.

'Let's be off!' cried Prince Osbert lightly; 'we have had enough of this now. Let the woman wiseacres in Parliament settle this little matter among themselves: it will afford them much satisfaction, I'll warrant.'

'Parliament!' echoed the Emperor, while his face turned very white. 'Surely not: this trifle is unworthy serious consideration. It would ill become our wise Senate if it occupied itself with the consideration of a woman's silly nonsense. I will, myself, settle this matter with Mistress Mercia. I promise that, gentlemen, so do not trouble yourselves further about it.'

'It shall not end in this way;' returned Geometrus firmly; 'I shall see that this matter is not hushed up.'

'So shall I!' came from a voice from behind a screen in the room; when therefrom emerged an old man named Sadbag, a leading Radical politician, who was dead against Royalty, and affected reform, advocating strongly a Republican form of Government.

'The Emperor's conduct is a disgrace to

our civilisation,' he continued, ' I have seen the beginning and end of the whole affair: for I was seated reading in that corner yonder, awaiting an audience of Mistress Mercia, when the Emperor was ushered in unnoticed by me; I continued reading until I dropped asleep and was aroused by the Emperor's passionate tones when making his love-appeals to the obdurate Mistress Mercia. She scorned him, and he got furious. I saw it all! I will never forget the scene if I live to the age of Methuselah!'

' My stars, but Kate will make it hot for thee! She will have good cause for her jealousy this time, old man! I wouldn't be in thy shoes for a kingdom; fancy, the virtuous Felicitas caught corrupting his astronomer! Oh, my, this is funny!' cried the light-minded prince, who laughed heartily, at the thought of the scrape his cousin had got into.

' Funny isn't the word for it—it is atrocious—abominable! It hath been ever the custom of idle monarchs to fill up their time with seducing good women. The hunting is more keen when the lady is virtuous, and thereby the game made all the more delightful. Let's do away with such good-for-naughts—they are a disgrace to our country!' cried the old man excitedly addressing Geometrus.

'So then, wouldst thou trump up a story to lose me my crown in order to establish thine own political absurdities? Thou, and the woman Mercia are in league against me! You twain have hatched this conspiracy to work my disgrace. But I will scatter it to the winds—I will prove its utter falsity. I will show how futile are your plans to bring about a revolution : Mercia and thou shall die for your crimes; for it is nothing short of high treason.'

'High bunkum, thy Majesty talkest!' retorted Sadbag sarcastically ; 'thy blundering only equals thy blustering. Thy cousin. the prince, and Geometrus are witnesses of the truth of my statement, for they saw for themselves the fag end of the affair ; they caught thee forcibly detaining the lady, and heard her threaten to kill thee.'

'That of itself makes high treason! To threaten the life of the Sovereign is enough—the law still holds good in my realms to

punish such crime with death.  This one
charge alone against Mercia is sufficient!  She
must die the death of a felon, and pay for her
temerity,' returned Felicitas, who thus inter-
preted the law with much assumption of
dignity, to suit his own convenience.

'The nation will not see Mercia die for
such a dastard as thou!' exclaimed Geometrus, suddenly awakening from the stupor of
surprise that had overtaken him, as the
matter developed itself.  'I saw thee last
week philandering around her, but at that
time I understood not its meaning; neither
did she; otherwise she would have taken
more precaution in receiving thee.  Even then,
she requested me to remain in the room when
she gave thee an audience.  She surely had
some instinct that thou wert not to be trusted
—ah—now I see it all!'

'A trusty witness truly!  She and thou
have spent the time philandering yourselves,
and this is why thou measureth me a peck out
of thine own bushel.  Thou shalt be indicted,
Geometrus, for breaking the oath of thine
engagement.  Thou hast been spending the
nation's time love-making, and hatching high

treason,—all three of you shall repent your little games.'

'Blacking the character of another will not clear thine own. These wholesale indictments of thine will not serve thee. Thy case is a poor one, and thou hadst better own thy fault, rather than invent outrageous charges against thine accusers;' urged the old man with greater calmness than he had hitherto displayed.

'Mercia made the admission herself,' replied Felicitas. 'She said she loved Geometrus and fain would marry him if she might.'

At this Geometrus started, and went very red in the face; being totally unprepared for this avowal of the Emperor; which gave him a sudden pleasure he was unable to conceal.

'There is proof abundant, if more be wanting, of the nature of the Emperor's business with Mercia,' observed Sadbag reflectively, then turning to the Emperor, he demanded—'What happened that this matter of Geometrus's love was discussed between you ?'

'She desired me to use my influence with my Cabinet to get the custom changed which hath been so long observed, so that she might retain her post and take a husband at the same time.'

'And thou, in thy great benevolence and generosity didst promise, and finish by trying to make her pay for the boon by accommodating thy desire?' suggested Sadbag, following up the clue the Emperor's admissions had given him.

'I will answer no more of thy questions, fellow,' responded Felicitas, who looking very uncomfortable made for the door.

'I think this business is getting too hot for thy Majesty ; thy capers are costing too dearly. What folly to count on a strong-minded woman like thine astronomer! Why didst thou not make advances to some idle lady of thy court where such favours are dispensed more readily?'

'I will have thee indicted for a revolutionist and a maker of mischief in my realms, and pay thee well for all these insults,' retorted the Emperor as he left the Observatory.

'Bounce and boast help no one for long ; not even an Emperor!' called out Sadbag after him.

## CHAPTER V

THE discussion then terminated, but not the dispute. Each went his own way with the determination to work out the discomfiture of his adversary, to the best of his ability. Sadbag made his way at once to his club, the headquarters of the Radical Association, and related the disgraceful occurrence to its leading members ; who realising the gravity of the situation convened a special meeting ; so that measures might be promptly taken to get first in the field in the exposure of the Emperor, and thereby nullify his evil intentions.

So perfect was the system of communication throughout the globe that the same evening, not only had the Radical newspapers the whole story set in type, but this society titbit appeared next morning on the breakfast tables of the people throughout the whole of the

Empire. As a matter of fact, two hours later the news was in every part of the world. It gave a splendid impetus to the trade, for each printing office turned out at least three times its usual quantity of newspapers for the first week, and double the number for every succeeding one the case lasted.

The subject for long enough furnished matter for light little articles in the monthlies, and heavy discourses in the quarterlies. It supplied the novelist with material for his plots, and the delighted dramatist for his plays. An Emperor on his knees to a subject was not an every day situation, while the scene where she threatens his life was quite too tragical to be neglected. It gave the libretto to the composer, great and small, of comic opera, and in serious opera it was thrilling. Mercia in a state of ecstatic bliss warbling sweetest love songs to the enchanted Emperor, formed a delicious scene that was irresistibly charming to all beholders. When the proper time arrived the fearless Sadbag sent a full description of the affair to every journal throughout the world. He even wrote it out, and telephoned the minutest details to India, and every country in communication telephonically, with the Teutonic Empire.

Therein the love scene was graphically described, in Sadbag's humorous vein, but with due regard to Mercia's sensitive feelings.

For the first time her personal character was given to the world, but such a halo of purity and modesty was drawn round it that it evoked everywhere the most enthusiastic admiration for her character.

The description of the Emperor's duplicity and contemptible meanness was given with ruthless vividness, when at the moment he was surprised, he endeavoured to turn the tables on the high-minded lady, who having proved invulnerable to all his blandishments he accused of having committed the capital offence of high treason.

From the commoner, to the crowned head of every country, almost, the story of the Emperor of the Teutonic Empire and his astronomer was discussed. In the cottage, the castle, the street corner, the court and the club, it became at once the leading subject of conversation.

' Ah, well ! ' observed one of the viceroys of Turkey—for that country had been long before divided between Russia, France and England—' this comes of giving women too much freedom : had it been a man that was filling the post of astronomer this could never have happened.'

' But it might to his wife ! ' answered one,

' With a different result,' added another ;

' Is then a married woman more compliant than a single ? ' queried a third.

' It all depends upon the sort of woman,' observed a fourth.

' The danger is lessened when the lady already runs a nursery,' remarked his neighbour cynically.

' Science meets that difficulty,' interpolated another of the party.

' A husband's jealousy is the greatest of all dangers,' retorted his neighbour.

' Cease these pleasantries, gentlemen, and discuss the matter seriously,' exclaimed an elderly minister with dignity, ' England is to be indeed congratulated on having women of such stamp as the peerless and incorruptible Mercia.  Search the world through and we shall be unable to find any to compare with them in physique, or mental attainments. They are indeed, Nature's queens, and in every way fit to grace a coronet.'

'Talking of coronets reminds one of crowns: there's a pretty hubbub going on just now; India expects to win her freedom and is casting about for an Emperor,' remarked another;

'Why not give it to Mercia, she's as good as a man?' suggested his neighbour.

'Better, I should say,' rejoined another of the group, 'judging from results.'

'The natives would never stand it: every nabob wants it for himself.'

'All cannot have it, that is very clear,' remarked one of the party.

'Better settle the matter by giving it to none of them, and choose a good stock from the country that ruled them, and made them what they are; and thus establish a Royal Line which will do them credit for all time,' suggested the elderly minister, who was a Frenchman and a believer in women, and especially a believer in the beautiful Mercia.

# CHAPTER VI

WE must leave these gentlemen in the far
East, and come back to Greenwich.

While the Emperor was returning to
London he cast about in his mind for some
way out of his difficulty.

He felt it was little use seeking the assistance of his royal consort, Catherine, daughter
of Nicholas of Russia.

She would have little sympathy with him
in his trouble, unless he could persuade her of
his innocence of the charges that were being
made against him.

Taking into consideration, too, that on
that very morning he had quarrelled with her,
and brutally told her that he heartily wished
himself rid of her, it was at present, scarcely
wisdom to seek her advice.

While his mind was thus filled with gloomy
thoughts, the silence was broken by Prince

Osbert who was accompanying him to the palace.

'Here's a pretty pickle, to be sure!' exclaimed the prince, 'a nice position for a royal Emperor to be found interfering with his lady astronomer, and she threatening his life to make him release her. What thou canst do to re-establish thy reputation is about as clear as mud to me, for by my conscience, I cannot see a way at all!'

'What a prating fool thou art, Osbert! I can plainly see unless thy tongue is kept from wagging thou wilt ruin me by thy talk. Say nothing at all about the lady having been detained by me. I don't mean to own to that part of it. Let us declare that she deliberately turned upon me when I expostulated with her upon her idleness; that will give the matter a better appearance.'

'Aye, truly, a better one for thee! But thinkest thou, cousin, that the House will believe thee? I guess, they will sooner take Mercia's word: remember its lady members, how bravely they defend their sex at all times. I wouldn't give a sixpence for thy reputation after they have handled thy case.'

'What care I for the good opinion of a handful of women? What are they in my vast dominions? Nothing, truly, nothing! Nevertheless, a monarch's virtue, should be, like Cæsar's wife, above suspicion: so Osbert, good cousin, thou must help me in this matter, and swear to all I tell thee.'

'Commit perjury! No thanks, not if I know it. I cannot tell a lie—I'm another Juvenile Washington. Besides, Felicitas, it goes against the grain to do a dirty trick to any lady, least of all, our peerless Mercia.

'She is a lady of untarnished reputation, with whom I would strongly recommend thee to make thy peace. Indeed, the ways of Emperors with their lady-subjects are quite too much for me—I cannot comprehend them.'

'Heartless, thou ever wert, Osbert, pray try to realise my situation, and give up thy attitudes and play-acting proclivities. Now, remember, I had no hold on her person, when you two dropped upon us—I was merely expostulating with her.'

'I'll have nothing to do with the matter at all, I shall say I was seized with sudden blindness at that moment and saw nothing.'

' Idiot, wilt thou keep to that ? ' inquired Felicitas gloomily.

' Yes, I will stick to that, wild horses shall not drag other from me.'

' No one will believe thee.'

' No one would believe the other thing, so it comes to the same for thee,' returned Osbert lightly.

' What other thing ? ' inquired Felicitas.

' Thy statement that she was idle, and thou wert reproving her for it. Her work proves her industry: she has any amount to show in defence of thy charge. Look at her maps ; her writings ; her daily announcements ; her daily registrations of her observations. The charge of idleness, I fear me, will not help thy cause.'

' It was not idleness in general, but some information in particular that she failed to supply me with.'

' Think it over, cousin, of what this particular information consisted. I bet my garters it was somewhat thou canst not explain publicly.'

' Cease thy chatter, and stick to thy resolve of having turned blind that very moment ;

'tis the best thou canst do for me, I see very plainly.'

'So I see, too, and as we two see alike we cannot come to any difference. Adieu, cousin, I hope Kate will not chide thee for having eyes for other women! That is my best wish for thee, this fine day.'

'I don't think that fellow could think seriously for five minutes if he had to be hanged for it,' the Emperor muttered to himself, using the old expression 'hanged' for it was still retained, although that form of execution had been given up long before.

As the Emperor was being driven back to the city, Prince Osbert who cared little for his company at this moment, alighted from the carriage, leaving him to the management of his own affairs. Felicitas, then promptly decided upon driving to the official residence of his prime minister, Mr. Stonesack, for he was anxious to confer with him concerning the dilemma in which he was placed. Moreover, he desired to intimate to his minister that steps must be taken at once for the arrest of Sadbag and Geometrus. Neither could Mercia be left out of the indictment,

for according to his story, she was the principal aggressor. He was not so lost to all
good feeling that he experienced no pangs
of self-reproach for the part he was taking
against the innocent girl; but he could see
only two ways out of the difficulty; either
the impeachment of Mercia and her friends,
or a full confession of his own conduct.

This latter would have been intolerable.
The deliberate exposure of himself to the
public, and a big public it was, by this time,
for it embraced the whole world, after having
so long played the part of Simon Pure to
popular opinion, was out of the question.
He would certainly shield himself, he thought,
and if the worst came to Mercia he could
exercise his royal clemency on her behalf,
and set her at liberty again.

By this course he would get rid of the
detestable Sadbag for good, and Geometrus at
the same time. Who knows, thought Felicitas
with a faint smile, but Mercia may still prove
kind to me, if that fellow were only put out
of reach.

Then followed in his mind bright visions
of a lovely dwelling, situated in some distant

part of his dominions, with Mercia for its mistress, and himself its secret owner, and constant visitor. How delightful! It should be fitted up like fairyland itself, with every luxury, and every appliance for her comfort. Little children might play about his knees, of which there was poor prospect of ever seeing in his royal palace; for so far, the Empress had proved barren. Then he awoke from his dream to the provoking reality of his true situation.

This pleasing reverie created, to some extent, a reaction in his mind. As his temper cooled so did his courage to make this heinous charge against innocent persons: but he supported himself with the reflection that at most the unfortunate men could receive no greater punishment than a term of imprisonment.

By the time his carriage reached the prime minister's residence he had decided what to say, for he had succeeded in inventing an excellent excuse for his visit to the Observatory.

He realised that it was necessary to have his statement ready as to the precise nature of the work he had requested his astronomer to prepare for him, which through her neglect had caused the extraordinary scene of which the prince had been an accidental witness.

After much cogitation he evolved the feasible explanation that he had requested her to make calculations of each perturbation of the sun's centre; and also to discover to what extent the additions of meteoric matter to his body would affect solar heat. He desired this information in the interests of all his subjects, but especially in those of agriculturists, and fruitculturists, whose crops had been ruined by the continuous cold seasons.

Under ordinary circumstances the Emperor would have obtained the attendance of any of his ministers without leaving his apartment; in one instant the summons would have reached him, had the minister been there to receive it.

Here was the difficulty, however, for delay increased the danger, and allowed the enemy an advantage; accordingly the Emperor chose the less dignified but safer course of calling in person on his minister.

While Felicitas was relating his extraor-

dinary account of the conduct of their astronomer and the subsequent treatment he had
received from her friends, Stonesack's countenance was a study to behold.  At first he
appeared profoundly astonished; this gave
way to so many varying emotions that it was
impossible to say what was going on in his
mind, or guess what opinion he had formed
of the affair.  However, he listened very
gravely to the story, in which the Emperor's
powers of imagination had been considerably
called upon.  And when the minister was
pressed for an answer as to the best method
of dealing with the delinquents, he hesitated
considerably, coughed; looked very red; blew
his nose, and finished by saying he didn't
know.

' At all events,' urged the Emperor, ' this
revolutionary Sadbag, ought to be indicted
for wickedly conspiring to undermine my
reputation, and thereby bring me into my
people's disfavour.'

' What about thy two astronomers, does
thy Majesty desire to include them in the
indictment? '

' Certainly,' replied the Emperor, ' did not

Mistress Mercia threaten my life with her ebony life-preserver, and hath not Geometrus taken her part?'

'Hath thy Majesty fully considered the merits of the case, that it be a sound one; otherwise it had better not be gone into publicly at all. Would it not be far wiser to administer correction to these foolish persons by requiring them to make an apology for their ill-behaviour?'

'That they will never do, I am assured! Their looks and language betrayed their evil designs towards me. Get a warrant sent quickly, and put them in prison without delay—even now they may be working me infinite mischief.'

'It will come to a trial in that case. What will the nation say? Will the people take thy word in preference to that of Mercia?'

'I care not what the people think! I know my own mind: I promised those seditious ones what to expect, and they shall not be disappointed,' returned the Emperor hotly.

'As thy Majesty wills it: the warrant shall be made out and served to-morrow. It cannot be done more quickly. In the meantime thy Majesty will have opportunity to sleep upon thy purpose, and if thy mind be changed by morning send a message to that effect, I will keep in readiness for it.'

'Count not upon that! There is no other way of dealing with those wretched conspirators,' replied Felicitas moodily.


While Felicitas was making his plans with the Prime Minister another member of the Cabinet was listening with astonishment to Geometrus' story; for Geometrus having travelled to the city in his own electric car made up for lost time by beating the Emperor's horses in rapidity. Consequently, he arrived at the official residence of the Chancellor of the Exchequer, or Minister of Finance, about the same moment as Felicitas at the Prime Minister's.

But Geometrus was not as well prepared with his statement as the Emperor. Moreover, he was unaccustomed at seeking audience of great people, and when he was ushered into the reception-hall of Lord Divesdale he felt exceedingly shy, scarcely knowing how to state his errand.

'My lord,' said he, and then stopped short, and blushed violently.

'Pray be seated,' said the minister in a kindly tone, for he was well acquainted with Geometrus, and had an excellent opinion of him.

'I have somewhat to tell thy lordship,' he commenced anew.

'What is it?' inquired Divesdale as he sank back in his armchair, in easy attitude.

'It concerns Mistress Mercia, the Astronomer Royal,' he managed to utter.

'Ah, whatever concerns Mistress Mercia interests me; for she holds my good opinion,' observed the minister smiling, and giving Geometrus a nod of encouragement to proceed.

'I am heartily glad to learn that,' rejoined Geometrus, recovering himself, 'for she stands in need of good assistance at this moment.'

'What is the matter—has she met with any serious accident?' inquired the minister in alarm.

'She has met with that which is infinitely harder to bear to one of her pure mind, than any physical injury.'

'Thou speakest in riddles—pray explain thyself?' returned his lordship a little sharply, for he was getting impatient.

'My mistress has been grossly insulted by one who has taken advantage of his high position,' Geometrus proceeded to say, but evidently with much reluctance.

'By whom—Prince Osbert?' queried his lordship hastily.

'No, my lord, the Emperor himself,' answered Geometrus in a low voice, but firm; the tones of which betrayed also the pain it cost him to make the disclosure.

'The Emperor!' repeated Lord Divesdale in profound amazement.

'The same,' Geometrus replied laconically.

'How—in what manner? Pray tell me in a reasonable way what thou knowest of it?' exclaimed Divesdale impatiently.

'The Emperor has been coming much of late to the Observatory. Last week he made a journey thither ostensibly to talk astronomy with Mistress Mercia. Yet I saw he looked annoyed at my entrance, and as if I had been an interruption to him. However, this day he came again, and as I was in the city at the time, he obtained good opportunity to say all he desired, presumably, for it finished with Mercia tearing herself out of his grasp and threatening to take his life if he detained her further.

'Prince Osbert, who had followed the Emperor to the Observatory for some purpose, entered the building at the same moment as myself, and we two suddenly came upon the scene just as Mercia had opened the door of the apartment to leave him. I looked into her face and saw it expressed the utmost scorn and indignation. "What is the meaning of this?" I asked, turning to the Emperor. "Oh, nothing," he replied; "she has forgotten a duty, and I am upbraiding her." "Liar!" exclaimed Mercia, "ask thine Empress to come hither, I have somewhat to tell her, and as for thee—find some other to fill my post, for I am thine astronomer no longer."

'Notwithstanding Mercia's indignant refutation the Emperor persisted with his charge against her of idleness, and disobedience to his command; when I told him plainly that the matter should be made subject of a public inquiry; for Mercia was too honourable and pure-minded to invent a foul charge against anyone, least of all her royal master.

'At this critical moment who should emerge from a corner of the apartment but Sadbag, the leading Radical member of Parliament? " I too, will take care that this be seen into!" he exclaimed. At this, the Emperor fumed furiously, and declared that it was all a plot against him, and he would have the three of us arrested for conspiring to defame his character; and finished by calling it high treason.'

'How utterly absurd of him! But how did Sadbag come to be there so conveniently? it is as good as a comedy, by Jove!'

' He explained that he was first in Mercia's reception-room awaiting an audience of her, and by chance taking up a book he became so interested in it that he finished by falling asleep over it, so that the entrance of the Emperor, and a moment later of Mercia, he was quite unconscious of; a screen stood between him and them, consequently his presence was unperceived: and he only became aware of theirs when the Emperor in impassioned tones pleaded his love suit with Mercia.

who disdained it. By that time Sadbag deemed it prudent to keep quiet, for he was getting more than he bargained, when he ensconced himself in the huge easy chair near the screen.'

'What a shocking old man to spy at a love scene! I wonder how he contained himself so long!' exclaimed Divesdale, who was bursting with merriment, for he ever saw the comic side of a thing, however grave it might be. 'The Emperor must apologise to fair Mercia, and to thee, too, Geometrus. Throw aside thy dignity, et cetera, and help to square this piece of business; it's no earthly use making a hue and cry over it. No lady cares to see herself a town talk! But this Sadbag—what are we to do with him? He truly is a sad bag of cranks! A piece of positive electricity, seeking its own level. not considering consequences; or a flash of forked lightning ready to put one on toast; or a match in a powder-box ready to pop —the man is in fact, too dangerous for any-thing.'

'He's the right man for the times! I'm not going to put the stopper on him. The

Emperor must be made an example of,' returned Geometrus fiercely.

'I hope not, by Jove! the peace of the community would be permanently spoilt, if we all followed his example,' observed his lordship drily.

'I mean that the Emperor should be made a warning to all light-minded persons, in general, and monarchs in particular.'

'Quite so: the Emperor by our endeavours shall be made more particular, especially in his treatment of the ladies.'

'And Sadbag is the right man to do it!' shouted Geometrus, who was getting quite warm with the discussion.

'He's a right man in the wrong hole! I mean he's got the Emperor in a queer hole, and he won't let him out of it! The position doth wholly delight him. He'll take a holy joy in "taking it out of him," or "putting him up a tree," or making him eat humble pie, or what thou likest! Oh, he's a sad dog or sadbag, I know not which, and no mistake! But we must circumvent him.'

'I have no desire to circumvent him; I would infinitely prefer to help him. I do not regard this affair in the same light as thou, and could have hushed it up without the aid of a Cabinet minister, for the Emperor desired the same on the spot, offering me promotion, but I refused it on such terms,' interposed Geometrus with much spirit.

' I would that all men were as thou art, my friend, for then there would be neither place-maker nor place-seeker. What a perfect Government we should have ; everyone seeking his neighbour's good to the detriment of his own ! The world indeed, would be too perfect for anything ! '

' No fear of that as long as there are those who strive to cover up ill-doing. I will seek Mr. Sadbag and get counsel of him, for it is very plain I can obtain no good advice from thee,' said Geometrus, who was altogether disgusted at the minister's light raillery, and rose from his seat to go away.

' Stay, I hear familiar footsteps ! One seeks admission whom I would see before thou leavest me,' exclaimed the minister, who despite all his playful talk, knew how to act most wisely.

· The Emperor ! Sire, thy visit is well-timed; one moment, in private, I beg,' and Divesdale conducted Felicitas into an inner apartment.

'I require thy help and advice in a most painful matter,' quoth the Emperor, turning very red in the face, but his speech was interrupted by the minister in a very offhand manner.

'Sire, not another word, I have heard the whole story—'tis a frightful hobble, I must say. Truly a most diverting drama! Beats broad burlesque to bits! If society should get hold of this precious piece of scandal thy prestige will be ruined! An Emperor is a god, or at least, a demigod, who should appear perfect before his people, whether he be or no. But, now, he must step down from his pedestal, and apologise, just to straighten things comfortably. Nay, it cannot be hard to kneel to a deity, for Mercia is no less! All beautiful women are goddesses, let down from the skies for our adoration: 'tis very plain they were created for man's worship: away, then, and fall down upon thy knees and implore her mercy.'

'But she will not hear me,' cried the

Emperor taken aback by this unexpected harangue; 'she is proud, haughty, and obdurate—ah, thou knowest not Mercia!'

'The woman never breathed who could turn a deaf ear to the man who entreated her properly. Only kneel metaphorically, but talk to her prettily, and gaze into her eyes with tenderest pathos, and she will melt with pure pity for thy condition.'

'I've done it all!' blurted the Emperor unwittingly. 'I mean it's no use, she is quite too hard-hearted to help me.'

'I was sure of it, Sire, thou hast done too much already,' exclaimed Divesdale, with the audacity that is engendered of close intimacy. I will myself entreat her to overlook thy naughty conduct, and thy charges against the two men must be withdrawn. By taking conciliatory measures the thing may blow over; but otherwise it may prove very unpleasant for thy Majesty.'

Thus with his raillery, for the Emperor and he were familiar friends, Divesdale had discovered the truth; and now knew for certain what the other minister only guessed at.

'Conciliatory measures!' repeated the Emperor, who had by this time recovered himself, and who knew that he had already gone too far to be able to retract with any show of respectability, 'impossible! She threatened my life, and my prime minister has commanded that a warrant be issued for her detention.'

'Surely thy Majesty cannot be in earnest?'

'I never was more so,' the Emperor answered with an assumption of haughtiness.

'What about Sadbag and Geometrus?'

'They too will get served with the same sauce,' replied Felicitas, with true autocratic audacity.

'Has the prime minister really advised this measure?' inquired Divesdale gravely.

'I have commanded it,' returned the Emperor sharply.

'On what grounds?'

'Conspiracy; the three had conspired to scandalise me, and take away my character.'

'And they'll do it too!' cried Divesdale, with his characteristic impulsiveness.

'They shall have the opportunity of

publicly doing what they were bent on privately.'

'He has turned dotty, I'm sure of it,' thought Divesdale, 'in a monarch a little madness is a great danger. Well,' said he aloud, 'thy Majesty hath chosen thine own course and must abide by it, for I will wash my hands of the affair.'

'Oh, wash away!' said Felicitas testily.

'Thine action against the two men is illegal: no warrant for their imprisonment can be issued: their fault is merely libel, and all Sovereigns are used to that!' interposed the minister drily.

'Thou makest a mistake there, friend,' answered the Emperor with a wise look, 'remember my royal mother, Victoria the Second, who led such a virtuous life and was so proud thereof, that when the " Times " newspaper published a paragraph announcing that she was about to marry her late husband's father she was so scandalised thereby that she caused an Act to be passed decreeing that anyone who uttered a serious scandal against the reigning Sovereign should be indicted for high treason, for she held that the good name of the Sovereign should be considered as sacred as their person; under this Act, therefore, are these two scandal-mongers to be arrested.'

'Ah, yes, I had forgotten it! But that trifle would not be scandal now. Only twelve months ago thy hand signed an Act permitting thy subjects to marry whom they will, save those in the first degree of consanguinity. A man may marry his grandmother now, if he choose!'

'Of course,' admitted the Emperor, 'only he does not choose, as a rule.'

'It is inadvisable from every point of view: nowadays one's grandmother attains such longevity that to marry her for her fortune, is like turning monk for a livelihood: a man's freedom arrives when 'tis not worth the having, for she goes on living until he becomes grey-headed.'

'True! But this is not my business!' broke in the Emperor impatiently, 'let us discuss what more nearly concerns me. Can I count on thy good service in this matter, or no?'

'Call a Cabinet Council,' suggested Divesdale, ' in the multitude of councillors we shall get wisdom,' he added, quoting from very ancient history.

The Emperor made a gesture of impatience at this sally, for he felt the minister was drawing him, and took his departure forthwith.

The thought instantly crossed the minister's mind that the affair would make a very interesting plot for his next novel; for he was a favourite novelist whose works were welcomed by the people for their merit, and not because they were written by a popular minister of the State.

'If we could only put the actual occurrences of life as they appear before our eyes into our works what rattling good stories we could write!' laughed Divesdale, as he threw himself into his easy chair for a smoke and a soliloquy.

Ideals of art and literature are as subject to change and remodelling as are theories of natural science, which are bound to give way as the light of knowledge reveals little by little the true conditions of the mysteries of life and its environments. Accordingly literature-making had its fashions ; a reaction had taken place, and from the field of novel writing which had been in the past almost entirely filled by lady writers, these were now self-eliminated ; women having successfully taken up the positions of historians, mathematicians, political economists, and expounders of natural and mental philosophies. So successful was the female in the writing of books designed for instruction that no male had a chance in this walk of literature, unless he assumed a feminine pen-name, and by this harmless subterfuge gain a reputation in spite of his sex.

Science as applied to manufactures had reached such perfection that the stones for building purposes were now manufactured, the stone quarries, as a matter of course, having almost given out. By a cunning admixture of chemically prepared material whose chief substance was composed of silicious sand brought from the pathless deserts by electric motive power, at a comparatively small expense, this granular quartz, or flint under certain conditions was reconverted into beautiful slabs of stone, of hard and enduring quality.

It was no uncommon sight to see whole streets, or terraces of handsome houses built apparently of blocks of glittering granite which sparkled bravely in the sunlight: nor were these imitations confined to one sort, for various marbles were so closely imitated, and withal so hard and enduring that the villas of the middle classes bore the appearance of veritable marble halls. Inside the walls were not papered, but finished with a dressing of apparently beautiful marble, while a wainscoting of richly embroidered silk velvet imparted an air of comfort to the rooms; a by no means unwelcome addition, for the climate of England, like the poor, is always with us.

# CHAPTER VII

WHEN Mercia retired to her private apartment she hardly knew whither she was going. At first she entered her usual sitting-room, then suddenly she made a turn and rushed into her bedchamber where making sure there could be no interruption she gave vent to the sorrow and indignation that filled her breast. in a passionate flood of tears. For even the twentieth-century woman was not illachrymable, being in this respect pretty much the same as the most remote of her feminine ancestors.

In a few moments, however, she recovered herself, and began to consider her situation, or rather her loss of situation, for she had inconsiderately thrown it up in the heat of her anger with the Emperor. Not for an instant did the thought cross her mind of withdrawing her resignation, or of making any attempt at reconciliation with the monarch. whose utterly heartless and cowardly conduct filled her with intense contempt, and disgust. As soon as the tumult of her feelings had subsided she returned to her sitting-room and wrote out her letter of resignation, wherein she explained in modest yet dignified terms her reasons for taking this step; expressing at the same time the terrible sacrifice it was costing her in thus throwing up a position which was so specially adapted to her sympathies and pursuits, and of which there was no hope of obtaining an adequate substitute elsewhere.

When the letter was completed she remembered Geometrus and wishful to satisfy him by making him fully acquainted with her movements she put it through the copying press with a view of showing him its contents : then ringing for a messenger it was despatched through the post without delay, that it might be received in due order by the head of the governmental department.

Having gone thus far she began to feel more settled in her mind, satisfied insomuch that she felt she had done the right thing in resigning a position which exposed her to the importunities of a patron who had proved as unprincipled in purpose as he was sensual in inclinations. Then she began to torment herself with the reflection that she had not proved such an icewoman as she had previously imagined herself to be. 'Yes,' she owned to herself, 'there was a moment when the power of his passion moved me, and I could have yielded to the seduction of the senses, pictured by him as the essence of love, until I remembered there was a barrier that might not be moved; no, not for the allurements of a century of deliciousness would I defraud another of one iota of the affection which was sworn for all time to be hers.

'I have refused, perhaps, the crown of an Empress to take the lowly condition of a poor scholar out of place; but I have remained true to myself, and to my sex, and before all things have kept my heart and hands clean : I have earned the approval of my conscience, and my night-pillow is not made restless with the self-torture of knowing I had inflicted an endless misery on another, and that other made like unto myself; with all the capacities of suffering, having to drink daily of life's bitterest mortifications.

'But what a deadly traitor I have narrowly escaped—what a contemptible monster he has proved himself, to thus turn on me like an adder!'

His threat of having her indicted for high treason gave her, however, no uneasiness, for it only inspired her with the utmost scorn. She dismissed it from her mind as having been on his part merely the outcome of ungovernable anger at being exposed before his enemy, as Sadbag undauntedly owned himself to be. How a man could express the most profound attachment for her at one moment, and seek her destruction at the next, seemed to her pure mind so monstrous and wholly unnatural that its possibility in her case was altogether out of the question.

That Felicitas would actually go the lengths of formally making such an infamous accusation she could not bring herself to believe. Thus she sat deeply pondering over the situation for at least two hours, unheeding the passage of time in which startling doings were taking place in the outside world, when

she was interrupted by a double announce-
ment, dinner, and the advent of Sadbag.

'In a brown study, I see!' exclaimed the
old man as he entered the apartment, 'can
I be of any use to thee?'

'Thrice welcome,' she answered quickly;
'this solitude is unbearable: I was longing
for some sympathising friend in whose ears I
could pour forth my trouble.'

'Thou art in a queer quandary, certainly,'
quoth Sadbag in gentle tones, which were not
wanting in sly humour, 'nevertheless, there
will be somebody in a bigger by to-morrow
morning.'

'To whom dost thou refer?'

'To Felicitas of course: the Emperor shall
learn ere another twenty-four hours the opinion
of the nation anent profligacy.'

'What hast thou done in this matter,
Master Sadbag,' said Mercia anxiously, 'pray
tell me, for only an hour ago I sent in my
resignation?'

'Sent thy resignation!' repeated Sadbag,
'why Mistress Mercia, there's no occasion for
that! It is the Figure Head Felicitas who
should resign; for having no worthy occupation to fill his time he must needs get into

mischief; in much the same manner as those empty-headed puppies who dawdle about the squares feasting their eyes on every comely woman who is on her way home from her office, or business. Down with the monarchy, I say, if this be all it is good for! Indeed, we have had enough of it. Look at the centuries of oppression that Russia has gone through! The country knew no real freedom until she shook off the thraldom of despotism and all its concomitant tyrannies.'

'Yes,' replied Mercia earnestly, 'Russia has attained the joys of a Constitutional Monarchy through rivers of human blood: devastating floods of fire, and seas of darkest misery: is it indeed worth the cost of such terrible sacrifices?'

'No great victory has ever been achieved save at infinite sacrifice. True, it was a mighty one, but the result is worthy of it. The struggle was long and severe; but greater severities have been put an end to—the cruelties of oppression wrought upon millions of helpless beings, which were accentuated by the conditions of civilisation and enlightenment that surrounded them.'

'Civilisation and enlightenment are of no avail unless the heart be true, and the conscience good. If the moral nature be at fault what avails the enlightenment of ages?' observed Mercia thoughtfully.

'The occurrences of to-day is a case in point,' continued Sadbag; 'in all history have we a parallel instance of meanness, cruelty, and downright dishonesty as this experience with the Emperor? But I have come to give thee good tidings—I think I have settled him. To-morrow the whole world will ring of his doings. His hypocrisy, his deceit, and his cowardice will make him the object of detestation to all. The four quarters of the earth have got the story word for word, and we shall see what comes of it.'

'Sadbag, what hast thou done?' demanded Mercia with eyes of fire and cheek of flame.

'Fear nothing, sweet lady, thy fair fame hath been kept guarded and unsullied by me. Not a word is given of which thou needest be ashamed. In this recital thou art truly pictured; gentle, modest, and unsuspecting up to the point where knowledge is forced upon thee, and the deceiver shows his hand. Then,

the art of the seducer utterly fails in its purpose, for thine irreproachable virtue shielded
thee as a coat of armour ; thy sense of honour
to thy fellow-woman was as a wall of defence
to thy shoulders, for thou didst refuse the
most tempting blandishments rather than
blight the happiness of a wife; albeit thou
wert offered the crown of an Empress as the
reward of thy dishonour.  But what of thy
letter of resignation; I wish I had seen it
beforehand ; for the Emperor makes a bitter
enemy, and will revile thee soundly to his
ministers ? '

‘ I think I have made myself pretty clear,’
replied Mercia, who had considerably calmed
down by this time ; ‘ here is a copy of my
letter ; read it.’

‘ Good ! ’ exclaimed Sadbag as soon as he
had finished perusing the document ; ‘ this is
fine !  Canst thou trust it with me for one
night and I will return it to-morrow morning
without fail ? ’

‘ Seeing thou hast done so much already,’
returned Mercia in a weary tone of voice,
‘ there can be no harm in giving it thee to
make what use thou mayest choose.  But,

listen, here comes Geometrus—I will invite
him to dine with us, and we three will discuss
the matter together.'

At the next moment Geometrus had entered
the apartment, and startled the two with the
look of painful concern on his countenance.

'Why so glum, my friend?' cried Sadbag
cheerily; 'this is but a passing cloud which
will be carried away presently by the fair
breezes of public opinion. No one can hurt
thee, or Mercia: I cannot say so much for
myself, for indeed I have meddled considerably
in this business, and nobody knows how it
will turn out for me. But ye twain are innocent victims, and have naught to fear in this
advanced period of the world's history. Truth
and justice should prevail in the dawn of the
twenty-first century, if ever it is to prevail at
all on this earth. Ah, I wonder if anything
approaching perfection can ever be reached
here!'

'Our present day littérateurs,' observed
Mercia, 'felicitate themselves that we are in
the enjoyment of such an advanced civilisation
as the world has never seen in the past, or
possible to attain in the future. But thou,

Sadbag, seest much to improve in the political
arena, and I see much to be discovered in
the world of Nature. We have still to learn
how to rule the elements. As yet, the winds
and the storms, and the waters, are our
masters. The time will arrive when these
shall be our servants to come and go at our
will. The rains it is true now water the earth
at our desire, but soon the winds shall be
dispersed by our art, and the heaving waves
of the ocean shall be made subservient to our
will; not by the wand of the sorcerer, but by
the hand of that more wonderful magician—
Science. When man has made Nature to obey
his behests then that extraordinary time shall
have arrived that the prophets dreamed of in
the far-off ages, which they symbolised by the
metaphor of the lion and the lamb lying side
by side. This, indeed, is the true millennium
for which all may ardently pray; for it is
the earth-glory awaiting the planet-dwellers
of our sun's system, yea, of every star system
throughout the whole of the vast universe.'

Mercia paused, and looked at her friends,
as if inquiring if she might proceed.

'Go on,' said Sadbag, 'we delight to listen to thee.'

'Ah, it is all very wonderful! The field of science possesses still untrodden paths: mystery upon mystery are yet to be made clear; the hidden secrets of psychology are still in darkness; we know not of what stuff we are made. What is soul—what is mind? We cannot definitely define them: we know only the manner in which these express themselves to our physical nature: the spiritual is wrapped in impenetrable mystery. How is it that one man utters the truths of a prophet, and another can hardly be made to understand what is going on before his eyes? Of course it is a difference in brain-power, the physiologist tells us, but how is it that a more or less quantity of grey brain-substance can give inspiration, knowledge, genius, power, imagination, and even prescience? Who can answer that? When this question is solved then is the chief millennium reached.'

'Let me have a word now,' said Sadbag, whose eyes glistened with the enthusiasm that inspired him for the moment; 'when the insignia of Royalty is done away with; when

kings are a luxury of the past, and Emperors
are persons of bygone history; when liberty
and equality are recognised everywhere; when
exorbitant taxes are no longer levied on the
poor; when society recognises the duty of
honesty and purity towards each other, and
the golden rule is abided by, then is the
millennium! Each of us has his goal, his ideal;
this is my ideal, and this is the religion I
would have preached by the expounders of
faiths, and of doctrines. Scientific discoveries
are being made step by step, first this experiment, and then that. One man finds a glint
of light, and theorises on it, and he passes
away, and another takes it up and examines
it further, and presently discovers a wider
field of vision, and he has dreams of its utili-
sation, but they end there; and a third,
having had an excellent foundation to start
with, finishes by discovering how to apply the
knowledge to useful purposes, and gains the
reward; for the first sowed, and the last
reaped; and he will give his name to the
invention, and will be hailed as the great
genius, the true discoverer.'

'Yes,' observed Mercia in reply to her

guest, as seated at table she dispensed her hospitalities with thoughtful care, 'they are all links in one great chain, one following the other in due order, displaying a complete system, which is governed by fixed laws, that may not be transgressed without penalty. But, say, Geometrus,' uttered Mercia anxiously, 'how has it fared with thee—why art thou so melancholy?'

'I cannot help it,' he answered, sighing deeply the while; 'a great misfortune is overshadowing the three of us.'

Mercia regarded him earnestly. 'What is it?' she asked.

'The Emperor's threat, I'll be bound!' growled out Sadbag.

'The same,' answered Geometrus gloomily; 'I have just come from Divesdale, the Minister of Finance, who was having converse with the Emperor upon the subject, and he tells me Felicitas is bent upon punishing us, yea, the whole three—even Mercia is not to be spared.'

'Yea, rather he is working the punishment that's to fall on his own pate!' laughed Sadbag contemptuously. 'When the proper time comes I possess indisputable proof to show in open court of the truth of my statement, which will place that of Mercia beyond doubt also; and thou, Geometrus, being only an accessory in the affair, and not a chief actor, when we are cleared thou wilt be also. Be assured this bogus prosecution will be promptly stopped unless we insist on its full development.'

'And where wilt thou obtain all this convincing evidence? There's naught but our bare word to support our statements: the highest potentate of the realm and the policeman can never swear falsely?' remarked Mercia, cynically, who was awakening to the gravity of the situation.

'We shall be arrested to-morrow, at latest,' interpolated the young man, 'the warrants are being made out at this moment.'

'Capital!' shouted the elder man, slapping his knee exultingly, 'I wouldn't miss the scene at the trial for a kingdom!'

'Oh, Sadbag, thou art horrid!' cried Mercia deprecatingly, 'I shall never survive the disgrace of it!'

'Say, rather, thou wilt be too shy to survive the honour of it! Mercia, mark me, the day of thy trial will be the dawn of thy glory. Truth will triumph this time, notwithstanding the world's wickedness. The words of our ancient Solomon shall be verified—" A virtuous woman is as a crown to her husband," et cetera ; ' and Sadbag looked slily at Geometrus, for an irrepressible humour was ever bubbling up within him.

'But I haven't a husband,' murmured Mercia, blushingly, ' so how can I thus adorn him ? '

'The man and the opportunity are awaiting thee : the one at thy elbow, the other looming near,' explained Sadbag archly.

It was Geometrus's turn to blush now, which he did most becomingly,—'If Sadbag means me,' he faltered out, ' I would fain be the man, I confess ; but where is the opportunity ?  It seems to me that it was never so distant as at present, and it was at all times too far to give hope.'

' Modesty doth well become youth, but it is ill-placed in cases of the heart.  He that is daring gains the goal, but the fainthearted gives up the race.  It is true ye twain are in a predicament, having lost your appointments, but you are no worse off than if this misfortune had never befallen you, for marriage would have brought a like result. I propose,' Sadbag proceeded to say, ' that thou Geometrus shalt ask Divesdale for the appointment of Head of the Royal College of Natural Science, where thou wilt have power to appoint all its various professors, and lecturers. As astronomy is one of the principal subjects taught, give Mercia the post of Chief Astronomical Lecturer, which carries no bar to marriage. Now isn't that plan most excellent! I flatter myself it is a capital thought!'

'It's splendid, yet it possesses a fault!' exclaimed Geometrus, whose spirits began to rise at the bright prospect held before him: 'could not Mercia ask Divesdale for the appointment of Principal, and give me the subordinate position of Professor?'

'Whichever way you two choose to put it,' replied Sadbag merrily; ' after all, when I come to consider it I believe Mercia would stand the better chance with the minister: the nation at large, too, would be more satisfied, as she hath renown and much goodwill of the people.'

'I feel as if I were already installed, and

am longing to award places of honour to all my friends,' broke in Mercia sweetly. 'What post, dear Sadbag, can I give thee? Political Expounder, or Professor of Economics? Name the article and it shall be forthcoming; for I fain would testify my gratitude for the honest goodwill thou dost show me.'

'I want naught for myself,' replied the old man with a comic shake of the head, 'but I have a grand-daughter ready to leave school whom I would wish to enter the said College as a student. It would much oblige me if thou wouldst examine her and judge for which science she is best fitted. She must select one subject and bottom it thoroughly; I think chemistry to be the most preferable.'

'Chemistry!' repeated Mercia smiling, 'why my dear sir, that's a very big order, for it possesses several important branches, each one a study of itself. One should be selected, and then there's a possibility of imparting something useful to thy grand-daughter. Nowadays no one has a chance of success if he attempt too much—this is the day of the Specialist!'

'It isn't every day one has a chance of a

good talk with a lady of such renown as thee, so I will benefit myself by taking the opportunity,' remarked Sadbag in a tone of great content; 'I have a grandson also, what shall I do with him?'

'How old is he?' inquired Geometrus, who thought it was time to put in an oar.

'Sixteen, and as comely a youth as ever was seen. But he has no liking for abstruse studies, and it is little use sending him to college with his sister. Can you suggest something that is likely to prove agreeable to his cast of mind?'

'Article him to a marble manufacturer,' replied Geometrus eagerly; 'it is the grandest trade going. We want marbles and granites for every building, nowadays; we cannot obtain enough of them. There is plenty of scope for further invention, for instance, porphyry has not yet been successfully imitated but in appearance only, for it is too brittle for any purpose necessitating strength and durability. A new "Stone Age" is dawning, for not a brick will be used save in the cottage of the poorest. Our large towns and cities will present greater beauty than classic Italy saw in its best days; for they will be filled with splendid halls and residences built apparently of various rare and costly marbles, designed in high artistic form and stately structure. What a wonderful age we are coming to, when the distant sands of Sahara are brought to our shores and reconverted to their original solidity! It is like a fairy tale of ancient days this transformation of the crumbled rock of ages to the original compactness of solid blocks of glittering stone. Who is the sorcerer of the modern time? The Geological-Chemist.

'Diamond making is as nothing compared with this useful manufacture, for it converts the ugliness of cheap brick buildings into the beauties of palaces. Even the sea sand on our own shores are cleansed and united with chemically prepared material, and made to form a hard and impenetrable silicious stone, more enduring than what it was in its pristine solidity.'

Sadbag looked serious as Geometrus dilated on the usefulness of Geologic-chemistry; then he remarked—'I imagined that chemistry had attained its limits, and further im-

provements in manufactures impossible, almost, but I see with your eyes, Geometrus.
and quite understand that the world is still in
its infancy, although it believes it is acquainted
with everything already.'

'So they thought a hundred years ago!'
observed Geometrus laughingly; 'the people
of that time actually imagined they had
scaled the extreme heights of knowledge and
there was nothing left to learn.   But hark!'
he exclaimed in an excited undertone, 'there's
a ring at the great door—who comes at this
hour?   Is it the warrants, I wonder!   It is.
There are the police,' continued he as he rose
and looked through the window, 'and the
police-van ready to accommodate us!  Oh.
Mercia is it possible that thou must suffer
this degradation?'

'SHE SHALL NOT!' exclaimed Sadbag
vehemently, 'as long as there's a breath left
in this body of mine.  My first thought was
to fly,' he continued hurriedly, 'on account of
this copy of her letter which I was about
sending to the Press for publication; but I
will hide it in this vase instead, and get my

solicitor to fetch it away afterwards; for I will now stand my ground for Mercia's sake. She shall be conveyed to prison in her own carriage, or not at all, there's no law to hinder that, I warrant. We three shall all go together, but I would have preferred my liberty a little longer for I have much to do before getting my incarceration.'

'Hide behind the screen again!' whispered Mercia, 'no one knows thou art here; it is easy enough to do; and thou canst report upon the manner in which I am treated, if need be—dost understand?'

'Perfectly, I will do it, and come out if I see necessary,' agreed the old man with a roguish beam in his eyes, while he slipped behind in a twinkle. He had no sooner disappeared than the constables entered the apartment, which they did in a somewhat hesitating manner. Evidently, they did not at all relish their work, for the inmates of the Observatory, as well as the place itself inspired them with respect.

'Why this intrusion on a lady in her private apartment?' demanded Geometrus haughtily; for he considered they ought to have remained in the entrance hall, until their errand was explained.

'What is your wish?' inquired Mercia in quiet tones.

'Mistress, I have brought with me a document, an ugly document, truly, to show a lady, and to such a one as thou it is indeed vexatious to have the handling of it. Nevertheless, it has been entrusted to me, and obedience is the first great principle of all order. Therefore, very unwillingly, I confess, I call upon thee in the Emperor's name to surrender thyself—here is my authority,' and he held out the warrant for her perusal, still keeping his hold of it. When she had finished, she stood for a moment thinking, whereupon he stepped forward to lead her away, when Mercia falling back a little, drew herself up haughtily, and exclaimed—'Touch me not. fellow, I will leave this house of mine own accord when I am fully prepared for my journey, for I must attire myself suitably before going into the night air, also my carriage must be made ready for me.'

'We have brought the ordinary police-van by special order of the Emperor, we dare not let any other be used,' interpolated another officer, for there were three of them.

'The police-van for *me*!' repeated Mercia indignantly, 'and by the Emperor's orders too! What has the Emperor to do with the administration of the law? I refuse to obey such an order.'

'And rightly so,' interjected Geometrus hotly, then turning with furious face upon the constables, he added—'This lady goes with you in her own carriage, or not at all.'

'What is that to thee?' returned the sergeant of police sharply, 'a pretty person to lay down conditions to us, and dictate how we are to perform our duty, seeing thou art in the same boat thyself. Here is the warrant for thy apprehension; and get thee ready quickly.'

'If you touch her, any of you, against her will, I will strike him dead with my electric dagger!' shouted Geometrus, who was beside himself with anger.

'There are more daggers than thine, young man,' exclaimed one of the men roughly, as he rushed towards Geometrus with his handcuffs opened ready to clasp them in an instant; but Geometrus was too quick for him, and tripping the constable with his foot, the latter staggered to the ground awkwardly, while the handcuffs were dashed out of his grasp with a deft blow from Geometrus. Then the other two constables springing to the aid of their fellow took hold of Geometrus, one at either side, and a desperate struggle was about to commence, but at this juncture out rushed Sadbag from his hiding place exclaiming—'Why all this bubbery, ye idiots, what matters it what sort of vehicle you use for their conveyance so that you get your prisoners safe in quod? That is enough for you! Let the lady go as she will, and no more nonsense about it, otherwise I will make it pretty hot, both for you and your masters, afterwards.'

'Now this is mighty convenient!' said the sergeant dryly, for he held the warrant for Sadbag as well; 'we want thee also, my good fellow, and thou hast saved us much trouble by popping out to lecture us; thou couldst not repress thy speechifying instincts, even to save thy liberty! I arrest thee, Joseph Sadbag, in the name of the Emperor Felicitas!

Here is my authority,' and he pulled out of his side pocket the document for Sadbag's perusal.

'Oh, I know all about it,' answered the old man testily, 'I am willing enough to become thy prisoner only let it be done quietly and decently, for the Emperor will have sufficient to answer for without adding further insult to this lady. He has already done that which will disgust every decent minded person in his realms.'

' Let him take charge of his own business : 'tis his affair, and I will perform mine,' replied the sergeant doggedly.

'You might come to a compromise.' pleaded Sadbag in insinuating tones, ' I have saved you heaps of labour, trouble and exertion in lying in wait, and watching for me all over London by unexpectedly dropping myself into your hands. Show your gratitude, my friends, by letting Mistress Mercia take her seat in her own carriage, and one of your constables may accompany her, while this gentleman and myself will go in the police-van, with the remaining two of you. and we will pass our word of honour not to overpower you, and seek to escape.  Now are you satisfied?'

'Very well,' agreed the sergeant gruffly, 'we will take the offer—only make haste!'

'It is quite dark outside, Geometrus,' observed the old man, 'no one will be any the wiser as to who are the occupants of the van : I don't much matter it myself—nevertheless, I will sue the Government for damage to my reputation, for this act will accentuate the situation.'

'I care not for myself one whit,' returned the younger man in a pained tone; 'but I am heartily glad thou hast succeeded in saving Mercia such an unnecessary disgrace.'

'I hope we shan't be kept a month of Sundays in our cells, for I am simply dying to make my *dénouement* in court,' whispered Sadbag to his friend, as he nimbly tripped down the broad staircase that led to the entrance hall, with the policemen following at their heels.

'For the life of me I can't imagine what thou art driving at—what the deuce is thy *dénouement?*' inquired Geometrus impatiently.

'Qui vivra verra!' laughed Sadbag lightly:

· ·· "He that lives longest sees most;" I mean to create a diversion in court.'

'A diversion!' repeated the young man in dismay.

'Well, maybe that's not exactly the word for it; I am not a flowery phraser: I mean to create an impression that may prove a diversion, or a lesson, an example, a warning, a farce, a terror, a maxim, a moral, a proverb, a motto; a subject for comic cuts, for high art paintings; for pulpit sermons, stump orators, parsons, preachers, and petticoats to moralise on; 'twill be a lesson to perjurers, profligates, and hypocrites, generally; and at the finish each will say to his neighbour—What a capital dodge, I wonder no one ever thought of doing that before!' and the old fellow rubbed his hands in high glee, at the thought of his plan, the success of which he felt would amply repay him for all the inconveniences of his most inopportune confinement.

By this time Mercia's carriage was in readiness, for it only required a few minutes' attention to put it in working order, and soon the quartette, each under the influence of his own emotions, watched the light barouche roll quickly along the smooth macadamised roadway, for only heavy trams and waggons used the rails with which the principal streets and roads were provided, lighter vehicles not requiring such aids to locomotion.

'Farewell, my Mercia,' the young man had whispered in her ear, just before turning on the force; for the driver had taken the steering gear; 'be strong and of good hope, Sadbag is our saviour, we have nought to fear with his clear head and true heart to help us.'

'Surely the gods will help their own sister!' exclaimed Sadbag gallantly, as he raised his hat in making a last adieu. 'Wait till the lucky bag is presented thee for a dip, and thou wilt see what a prize comes to thy hand!'

# CHAPTER VIII

'As atom unto atom firmly lies,
  Obeying blindly that great law which makes
  Subservient even lifeless matter; wakes
  An energy, a force, whose hidden ties
  Bind animate or inanimate in wise
  True, order. . . .  Thus are we twain commingled. . .'
                              *Idylls, Legends and Lyrics.*

PERHAPS the most wonderful of all the discoveries of this period was that of psychomagnetic sympathy, or psychic-energy, which was found to pervade the nerve-centres of all human beings, in a greater or lesser degree. In all ages the unseen bond that linked mankind together, with more or less hidden force, had baffled the researches of psychologists, and physiologists to such a degree, that at length the pursuit was abandoned, and left for Charlatans to play with.

Each epoch of the world's history saw the development of some absurdity; but these were in reality the fructification of the seedling; or infant gropings after that higher knowledge which evidence the spiritual aspirations of the human soul.

In the very early stages of man's history we find him in full belief of fairies, gnomes, and hobgoblins, which eventually ripened into a literature and folklore dealing with their doings, of quite ample dimensions. And after all, who would like to make away with those delightful stories that inspired his imagination in childhood's days, filling his mind with awe and wonder, while yet it was all receptive, and when credulity was paramount?

Then followed the belief in the wizards, witch, and magician, who were held to have gotten their supernatural powers from the arch-magician, Satan, himself: and every ill that nature sent humanity was ascribed to the infernal agency of witchcraft.

In these days handsome incomes were occasionally realised by courtly magicians who unfolded the future to the high-born ladies that invoked their aid. Did not Anne Boleyn see her future husband in the magician's mirror, when quite a girl, and as yet she knew nothing of him? The scene of a masked ball in which King Henry the Eighth was the central figure, and all the people paying him courtly homage, was found reflected in the magic mirror, and the monarch pointed out as her future husband. Still time went rolling onwards bringing its developments of man's highest aspirations—the desire to fathom that mystery of which he caught but a glimmering.

Then followed Mesmer's discovery to which was attributed certain psychological developments; these the Charlatan utilised to his own advantage by claiming the power of second sight for some fair sleeper whom he always took care to be provided with.

Side by side with mesmerism grew another new idea which went infinitely further than the mesmerised thought-reader. It was named Spiritualism, the votaries of which professed to call up at will the departed spirits of friends, enemies, and even of persons unknown to them in life.

This new faith, for it developed into a religion seeing that once a person got thoroughly soaked with it he wanted no church to teach him the way to Heaven, he believing he had found a more direct passage than what all the parsons in Christendom could show him.

Revelations from Spirit-land were sought not only by the lower, and partially educated classes, but also by the educated members of society; practical business men being found in considerable numbers attending spirit-rapping circles. Even the editor of the *Times* newspaper in 1880 was claimed by the Spiritualists to be one of them.

Eventually, Spiritualism becoming unpopular by reason of its adoption by the ignorant, together with the numerous exposures of fraud on the part of its leading exponents, a new belief was found necessary for the intellectual and cultured ones of the nineteenth century.

This was borrowed from the East, the beliefs of Ancient India being pressed into service and made to appear under a new form and given the title of Theosophy.

The whole series of superstitions under whatever name they might appear—witchcraft, fortune-telling, mesmerism, spirit rapping, Mahatma power, or the new-fangled faith of Theosophy, were in reality the deep workings of the human mind, striving to fathom the secrets of nature.

The physiology and psychology of the twenty-first century explained it. It was indeed, simple enough, for everything is easy when you know it.

It was found that a subtle fluid somewhat of the nature of electricity, which was altogether imperceptible to sight, but whose presence was indicated by a very delicate gauge called a psychometer pervaded the nerve centres of all human beings. It imparted to them such a highly sensitive condition that wherever the fluid was in great abundance it gave to its possessor a corresponding amount of attraction, or influence over others.

The influence of this essence was not limited to a short distance, for propinquity was not altogether necessary for its action; for a highly endowed person could throw out an invisible stream of psycho-magnetic sympathy that would find its way for hundreds of miles till it reached the corresponding fluid of the person desired, causing such a disturbance in his nerve-centres that immediately he would commence thinking of his friend, mistress, or acquaintance, as the case might be.

From this cause came into being that well known saying—'Talk of the Devil and he's sure to show himself.'

The poet in every age, although knowing nothing of physiology, being endowed with a superabundance of this wonderful essence, divined its existence, calling it the unseen chains that bound humanity together.

In fact, this was the source from which the true poet, novelist, orator, and thought-reader derived his power. All these were endowed bountifully with this subtle energy, putting it to the use for which their individual talents led them.

The actress who nightly enchained her auditory by her clever impersonation of some ideal character, did not owe her triumph solely to the influence of her splendid rhetoric, or histrionic art, but mainly to this force which she unconsciously scattered broadcast around her, the waves of which being caught up by the innumerable nerve-centres, which responded with ready receptivity.

The same force, but of a higher order, and more spiritual essence fired the imagination of the poet, giving him burning words, and tender sympathies that found their way into every heart.

It inspired him also with prophetic insight; giving him the power of seeing into the very heart of things, whether of the past, present, or future. The ancients saw this and averred that poets are born not made; for it was owing to the highly sensitive quality of this psychic energy that he possessed his gift of poesy.

It comes into the life of a few to meet with some exquisitely charming woman who excites love and admiration wherever she turns. All who come in contact with her unite in declaring her to be the sweetest woman that ever lived. No one can definitely tell you why she exercises so much charm over him; she is admittedly not more beautiful, nor more talented than others; nevertheless, she casts some indefinable, yet irresistible spell over all around her. Something unfathomable, unknowable dwells in her countenance, giving it an expression that haunts you. She sees into your very heart, as it were; she knows exactly what to say, and what to do to please and gratify you.

She utters your thought for you, expressing it so beautifully and perfectly that you are delighted with yourself, for she throws such a glamour over you that you imagine you have given the happy expression to the idea. What is this power she wields with such fascinating force? It is the subtle fluid that is unconsciously emanating from her. This secret, unseen energy profoundly stirs every nerve within you, sending thrills of pleasure through your frame, and imparting warmth and life, and love to all who come within its influence.

Little children love her, and nestle in her skirts; not only the animals of her own household, but the strange dog and cat look at her with longing eyes, wishful for the pat, and kind word that will certainly be granted. Each living thing feels the subtle influence and acknowledges it unhesitatingly. Sickness and suffering can hardly diminish it, for only death itself can annihilate it.

The orator holds his audience spell bound apparently, by his splendid eloquence; the whole audience which may consist of several thousands are moved by one great emotion. Every pulse beats as one; only one feeling pervades that vast assembly—perfect union of thought with the speaker. He is exercising a spell over the multitude powerful as that of the magician.

The following day the speech appears in cold print, and strange to say, there is nothing very remarkable about it. What was it that produced such deep emotions in the breast of that great concourse of people?

It was the wonderful influence of the speaker's personality; it was the abundant psychic-energy that spread itself in thought-waves all through the multitude, making their hearts glow and swell with happiness.

Such are the men who win great battles, for their soldiers are ready to rush into any danger under the influence of their leader's powerful soul-energy. Mark how these great warriors attract women. He who fights well, loves well, all chroniclers know that fact, and the unseen mind-force with which Nature has so lavishly endowed him, gives him the successful conquest of women's hearts, equally as of men's.

At this time thought-reading was a perfected science, and only those endowed with an extraordinary gift of psychic energy could pose with any measure of success as a professional.

So great was the perfection reached in this branch of science that a professor of thought-reading was expected to describe not only the thought of the inquirer, but also reveal the thoughts and motives of the person who formed the subject of the inquiry. Nothing less than this could satisfy the soul of the twenty-first century individual.

Once the Professor was placed *en rapport* with the person to be analysed and reported upon, he was expected to give every particular of his life, habits, attainments, thoughts and actions. In point of fact, he had to keep a mental diary of the watched man's doings. Woe betide the silly swain who tried to run two sweethearts; if one of them grew jealous she had but to tell her case to the thought-reader, and with a good fee set his brain agoing, when soon she would be in possession of every particular of her lover's perfidy.

As soon as the presence of this essence in all persons was clearly demonstrated and established, it became the ambition of the food-chemist to discover some phosphate that would increase the supply that nature had given already.  Numerous were the nostrums proposed for which were claimed the power of imparting an augmented supply to man.

The newspapers teemed with advertisements of these tabloids, some of which were frequently headed with the legend ' YE ARE NOT MEN BUT GODS!'  And indeed, if the virtues of these chemical preparations attained only half what was claimed for them, men would have been nearly gods by this time. For the inherent desire of man to obtain power, by whatever name it might be known, prompts him to accept any theories that promise this desirable gift.

For a time large fortunes were accumulated by the manufacture of psychic-energy tabloids ; enterprising chemists rivalling each other in the production of the most excellent. Notwithstanding all these deserving efforts on the part of mankind to raise himself, he remained pretty much the same as nature formed him, save by the slower processes of evolution.

Of all the persons who laid claim to the gift of thought-reading there was none so highly sensitive as the great Anglo-Indian, Dayanand Swami. It was said of him that he almost lived upon a wonderful elixir of his own manufacture, the preparation of which had been handed down to him from his Mahatma forefather some generations back.

In the solitude of the Indian jungle a hundred years previously his fore-elder had discovered this wonderful plant, which not only physically sustained him to a great extent, but furnished him with an extraordinary supply of the mystic fluid.

This ancient Mahatma was literally saturated with wisdom, without going through the painful processes that men of that class are usually compelled in the attainment of their ascetic ambition. By the agency of this psychic gift he could unfold, without having read its history, the glories of India in its ancient days; describing the magnificence of its rulers; their pomp; their immense retinues, which were on such a scale that the passage through his dominion by their Sovereign caused a famine in the parts traversed. Only two classes existed in those good old times, the very rich and the very poor.

He could conjure up pictures of the workmen dropping down dead from hunger and exhaustion who were engaged upon the erection of the loveliest mausoleum that the world has ever seen; more like an exquisite marble palace of fairy land than a resting place for the dead. Art had indeed attained its hightest perfection in those far off days, the monuments of which the Eastern still gazes upon with pride and affection.

Or he could project his thought till it reached the mind of ministers in England, when he could produce a mental negative, so to speak, of the thought of the ministers respecting the policy they intended carrying out which would affect India; for it was only on the occasion of some great national question stirring the mind of the people that he cared to put out his thought in this direction.

Moreover, he possessed the power of seeing into futurity, for he foretold that in one hundred years India would have her own supreme Sovereign, one who would be of their own unbiassed choice, who lived among them, and studied the happiness of her people. One who was loved and reverenced throughout the world. Whose rule would bring honour, dignity and renown to their beautiful and beloved India ; and this unrivalled potentate would be a woman, young, beautiful and talented.

Now, this prophecy of the old Mahatma could not refer to Victoria, the first English Empress of India, for she was gathered to her forefathers at that time, and King Albert, the First, reigned in her stead.

The descendant of this wonderful Mahatma resided in London, his father having been appointed by Government to the post of Col lector, a position of some importance in the Civil Service. But the son elected to follow a profession that was more in accordance with the traditions of his ancestors, and at the same time would supply a want in his own generation, that was called into existence by the exigencies of the times.

The worn-out theories of Theosophy which deemed nirvana the highest attainable condition of the human soul, had no attraction for him; but he regarded it with some amount of reverence, inspired by the traditions of an ancient religion, which cannot fail to cast a halo round it, even when discarded by the more advanced modern.

Dayanand Swami surrounded himself with the gorgeous luxuries of an Eastern prince, although dwelling in the English metropolis, and displayed his Eastern descent, by following Eastern customs as far as English conventionalities would permit. Nevertheless, he kept in touch with the times, accommodating himself to the requirements of the people among whom he had made his home.

The carriages of titled ladies might have been seen daily at his door; for love troubles, and court troubles disturbed the peace of great dames even in the twenty-first century.

Native servants waited obsequiously on these noble visitors who formed chiefly his *clientèle*, and whose rich fees sustained the splendours of his household.

Upon the arrival of a visitor the great door would be folded back, revealing a court-yard arranged in a style of true Eastern magnificence. The floor was formed of mosaics of elegant design cut from costly marbles. Shrubs, flowers, and trees of exotic birth filled convenient parterres, while a fountain played its crystal waters in feathery spray, giving the scene a refreshing sense of coolness. Birds of beautiful plumage disported themselves amongst the trees, adding colour, as well as life to the picture. The tiny humming-bird, like a moving flower-bud hung on the branches of beautiful shrubs, or basked in the sunshine of this artificial Eastern clime ; for the whole was covered with a high dome of glass of considerable area, which was supported by graceful pillars of manufactured marbles erected in regular succession. The tropical temperature obtained by the conservation of solar heat, being evenly sustained the year through, independently of the changes of weather.

The apartments within were arranged in

similarly luxurious style. The walls were hung with crimson satin, embroidered richly in gold, but the colours were varied according to the character of the apartments.

While the wall draperies of one room were composed of crimson satin, those of another were pale blue, another yellow, and so on, all of which were embroidered in richest hues, intermingled with gold. The couches and curiously carved stools were upholstered in rich materials that were in character with the decorations of the walls, and window draperies; while Persian carpets of the softest velvet pile sank like turf beneath the tread.

Costly ornaments of Eastern manufacture adorned the side tables, or were arranged on beautifully carved ivory brackets; while native Japanese paintings, encased in richest frames gave the *tout ensemble* a decidedly oriental appearance. The picturesque delineations of the Jap, whose ideas of art were totally different from those of the Western world, made their paintings real curiosities to the English mind. These represented lovers in nearly all stages of the *grande passion* seated in Japanese teahouses, or holding loving converse beneath the shade of luxurious trees, whose branches seemed to reach the deep blue skies. In another apartment portraits of great Eastern potentates, celebrated Hindus, and venerable Mahatmas gave the English visitor an idea of the former prestige of the Indian Empire.

In the lady's withdrawing-room containing the Japanese pictures, strains of sweetest music were set agoing at will, given apparently by a stringed band of automatic performers, made to imitate an orchestra of little men; who looked excruciatingly comic, as they moved their arms up and down, and waved about their funny little heads. The whole arrangement was set in motion by the same energy that gave heat to the apartments, conservatory, and cooking apparatus.

In his 'room of contemplation,' or studio, was daily seated at stated hours the highly gifted Swami, surrounded by his 'silent servants'—his books of Eastern lore. Tier upon tier of carved framework contained works from the most remote antiquity, dating backwards nearly four thousand years; and so on, through all the centuries, till quite up-to-date literature of the various epochs was represented. Rare manuscripts of the ancient Rig Veda, with plays, love stories, and fables, together with works on medicine, philosophy, mathematics, astronomy, and magic arts, all of very ancient date, filled the shelves of the library. While gorgeously-bound volumes of poetry, part of which were in the original Sanskrit, and part translated into English, were strewed on the elegantly designed coffee-tables, or stands, with which the drawing-room was furnished.

Here is a graphic description of the drought in an Indian summer, taken from a poem by Kâlidhâsa, of great antiquity, entitled—

*The Ritu-Sanhara, or, The Seasons.*[1]

> ' Now the burning summer sun
> Hath unchallenged empire won;
> And the scorching winds blow free
> Blighting every herb and tree.
> Should the longing exile try,
> Watching with a lover's eye
> Well-remembered scenes to trace—
> Vainly would he scan the place,
> For the dust with shrouding veil
> Wraps it in a mantle pale.

---

[1] Translated by Griffiths.

Lo, the lion,—forest king—
Through the wood is wandering ;
By the maddening thirst opprest
Ceaseless heaves his panting chest.
Though the elephant pass by
Scarcely turns his languid eye
Bleeding mouth and failing limb,
What is now his prey to him ?

Where the sparkling lake before
Filled its bed from shore to shore,
Roots and twisting fibres wind,
Dying fish in nets to bind ;
There the cranes in anguish seek
Water with the thirsty beak.

Elephants all mad with thirst
From the woods in fury burst :
From their mountain-caverns see
Buffaloes rush furiously.
With hanging tongue and foam-fleck'd hide,
Tossing high their nostrils wide,
Eager still their sides to cool
In the thick and shrunken pool.'

Here is an equally graphic description of
rain, from the same poem :—

' Who is this that driveth near,
Heralded by sounds of fear?
Red his flag the lightning's glare
Flashing through the murky air.
Pealing thunder for his drums—
Royally the monarch comes.
See ! he rides amid the crowd,
On his elephant of cloud
Marshalling his kingly train :
Welcome, oh, thou lord of rain.
Gathered clouds, as black as night
Hide the face of heaven from sight :

> Sailing on their airy road
> Sinking with their watery load.
> See, the peacocks hail the rain,
> Spreading wide their jewelled train,
> They will revel, dance and play
> In their wildest joy to-day.'

Coming down to a period as late as the twelfth century of our era were works representative of the Hindu poet of that time. Here is a translation of a poem, a pastoral drama, by Jayadeva, of which it is said ' the exquisite melody of the verse can only be appreciated by those who can enjoy the original Sanskrit.'

Krishna, the herdsman, loves Râdhâ, the shepherdess, but has wandered from her to amuse himself with other maidens. Nanda, Krishna's foster father, gives her warning, saying :—

> ' Go, gentle Râdhâ, seek thy wand'ring love;
> Dusk are the woodlands,—black the sky above.
> Bring thy dear wanderer home, and bid him rest
> His weary head upon thy faithful breast.'

Then Râdhâ makes anxious search for him, pressing through forest and tangled bushes, until a friend tells her in sheer pity that Krishna will not be found in lonely forest shades, and thus sings to her :—

' In this love-tide of spring, when the amorous breeze
  Has kissed itself sweet on the beautiful trees,
  And the humming of numberless bees, as they throng
  To the blossoming shrubs swells the kokila's song:—

' In this lovetide of spring when the spirit is glad,
  And the parted, yes, only the parted, are sad ;
  Thy lover, thy Krishna is dancing in glee
  With troops of young maidens forgetful of thee.
  Dispensing rich odours the sweet madhavi
  With its lover-like wreathings encircles the tree ;
  And oh, e'en a hermit must yield to the power—
  The ravishing scent of the malika flower.

       ' Saffron robes his body grace ;
        Flowery wreaths his limbs entwine ;
        There's a smile upon his face,
        And his ears with jewels shine.
            In that youthful company,
            Amorous felon ! revels he ;
            False to all—most false to thee.'

In the end Krishna, although faithless for a time, discovers the vanity of all other loves, and returns with sorrow and longing to his own darling Râdhâ.

In Swami's library were books containing collections of Hindu stories that had been handed down for hundreds of years, and repeated orally by each generation until at length various collections were made by native *littérateurs*, which sometimes were given very fanciful titles. Indeed, Hindu literature supplied the whole world with its stories, even the Persians stole from it considerably.

The following is an ancient Sanskrit love story by an author of repute, of the name of Subandhu. The chief beauties of this tale lie in its alliterations, double meaning of phrases, and puns, which bristle everywhere, all of which are of necessity lost in the translation. The plot is peculiar.

A king who lived somewhere on the Ganges, was a follower of Siva, and ruled his kingdom so admirably that impiety was unknown, proof by ordeal never needed, and violence never practised.

This king had a son, who was the delight of all who sought his protection, his sagacity always securing him from deception. His religious feeling was shown by marked devotion to cows, and to Brahmans ; and being comely as the god of love, (who by the way is furnished with his bow and arrows, showing that the idea may have been borrowed by the ancient Greeks,) he was admired by all maidens, far and near. The extraordinary fact, was however, that the maiden with whom alone he fell in love, was one that appeared to him in a dream.

He longed to dream again, but the fervour of his emotion prevented sleep.

He shut himself up in solitude, and refused nourishment. Then a faithful friend persuaded him that travelling might bring relief. They pursued their way to the Vindhya Hills; the sun was about to set as they entered a wilderness.

The friend collected roots and fruits, and the young prince fell asleep on a couch, made up of branches from the trees; but not for long. For he was awakened by the conversation of two birds who nestled in the jambu tree above him.

The female bird was reproaching the male for coming home so late, fearing that he must have been dangling after some other *sarikâ*. The male bird replies solemnly that he has been attending to a transaction most unprecedented.

He then relates that in the city of Kusumapura, (probably Patna) there is a lovely princess, named, Vasavadattâ. Being of full age, the king, her father, invited ' the highborn heirs of many principalities,' that she might choose a husband.

The suitors came, and the damsel took her place upon a daïs to survey them; but no one pleased her, and she and they withdrew in disappointment.

At night, the young prince who had fallen in love with her in a dream, appeared to her in a vision; and she felt at once that he was her destined husband.

The vision made known his name, which was Kandarpaketu; but she suffers torments of love and grief from not knowing how to meet with him.

Under these circumstances her confidante volunteers to go in search for him, and says the bird, she arrived here when I did, and is at this moment beneath our tree.

The lovesick prince no sooner heard this welcome intelligence than he introduced himself to the confidante, talked with her for twenty-four hours, (much too long, one would think) and then went with her to Kusumapura.

Here he found the lovely Vasavadattâ in a garden-house of ivory. On seeing each other they faint for joy, and afterwards rehearse their past sufferings.

The confidante speaks for the princess, and says that 'if the heavens were a tablet, the sea an inkstand, the longevous Brahma an amanuensis, and the king of serpents the narrator, only a trifling part of those agonies could be told.'

They next resolve on what we should call a 'runaway match;' and this they effect by mounting a magic steed which carries them to the Vindhya forests in the twinkling of an eye. They sleep soundly in a bower of flowery creepers, but when the sun is at meridian height the prince awakes, and finds Vasavadattá missing. He bitterly laments and wonders what can have caused so dreadful an affliction. Poor Vasavadattá having been the first to awaken, and seeing her bridegroom looking pale and emaciated. for the sickness of love had greatly reduced him, hastened away to gather fruits and food to restore him. In the midst of this loving occupation she was surprised by huntsmen and so frightened that eventually she lost her way, and found herself unable to return to her sorrowing bridegroom. After many dangers and difficulties were gone through.

the prince at length discovers her; she is conducted back to his father's palace, and they live in the greatest love and happiness ever after.

Carved upon the oak panels that lined the walls of Dayanand Swami's 'room of contemplation' were Sanskrit texts taken from THE RIG VEDA, the ancient Hindu Scriptures;

The portions selected had reference chiefly to the sun; the light of day being considered typical of the light of learning. The following are the English rendering of these short quotations from four thousand years old poems.

'HIS COURSERS BEAR ON HIGH THE DIVINE, ALL KNOWING SUN THAT HE MAY BE SEEN BY ALL WORLDS'

'AT THE APPROACH OF THE ALL ILLUMINATING SUN THE CONSTELLATIONS DEPART WITH THE NIGHT, LIKE THIEVES.'

'HIS ILLUMINATING RAYS BEHOLD MEN IN SUCCESSION LIKE BLAZING FIRES.'

'THOU OUTSTRIPPEST ALL IN SPEED; THOU ART VISIBLE TO ALL; THOU ART THE SOURCE OF LIGHT; THOU SHINEST THROUGHOUT THE ENTIRE FIRMAMENT.'

'THE DIVINE SAVITRI DISPLAYS HIS BANNER ON HIGH, DIFFUSING LIGHT THROUGH ALL WORLDS.'

'CONTEMPLATING ALL THINGS, THE SUN HAS FILLED HEAVEN AND EARTH AND THE FIRMAMENT WITH HIS RAYS.'

'THE TREMULOUS RAYS OF THE SUN THROW OFF THE DARKNESS, WHICH IS SPREAD LIKE A SKIN OVER THE FIRMAMENT.'

'OH, DIVINE SUN, THOU PROCEEDEST WITH MOST POWER-FUL HORSES, SPREADING THY WEB OF RAYS AND CUTTING DOWN THE BLACK ABODE OF NIGHT!'

These texts being carved in the original tongue—Sanskrit—Swami's English visitors were very little the wiser for having gazed upon them. Indeed, many persons imagined them to convey some deep mystic meaning that the great man would have been most unwilling to reveal. After all, if they could have looked over his shoulder and have seen how he spent his moments of relaxation, they would have discovered him perusing sundry very harmless works in his native language, for even collections of fables and fairy tales, which was a favourite form of literature in the East, served occasionally to relieve the weariness of his tired brain.

Here is a story of a Jaina ascetic, taken from a work named 'The Panchatantra,' a collection of fables and tales that long ago found their way into Persia. Nûshîrvân, the King of Persia sent a physician to India in search of medical knowledge and books; the physician not only brought back medical books, but collections of fables also, which, being translated into Pehlevi went forth to the world as the fables of Pilpay.

The book opens by stating that a certain king was concerned at finding that his sons were growing up without knowledge. He called a council at which the necessity of acquiring knowledge was discussed, and also the length of time required for the acquisition of such kinds of knowledge that was considered indispensable.

The conclusion at which the councillors arrived was that the king must be advised to entrust his sons to a Brahman named Vishnusarman, who undertook to teach them nîti in six months. This being arranged, Vishnusarman took the young princes to his house, and composed for their benefit a series of fables—the 'Panchatantra,' so called from 'pancha,' five, and 'tantra,' section—namely, five narratives. They are stories within stories, woven most intricately one within the other; here is a short one, treating of the cunning ascetic.

A certain king who reigned in Ayodhyâ,

the capital of Kosala, sent his minister to subdue a rebellion among some of the Rajahs in the hills. Whilst the minister was absent a religious mendicant came to Kosala, who by his skill in divination, his knowledge of hours, omens, aspects, and ascensions; his dexterity in solving numbers, answering questions, and detecting things covertly concealed, and his proficiency in all similar branches of knowledge, acquired such fame and influence that it might be said he had purchased the country, and it was his own.

The fame of this man at last reached the king, who sent for him, and found his conversation so agreeable that he wanted him constantly beside him. One day, however, the mendicant did not appear, and when he next came, he accounted for his absence by stating that he had been upon a visit to Paradise, and that the deities sent their compliments to the king. The king was simple enough to believe him and was filled with astonishment and delight.

His admiration of this marvellous faculty so engrossed his thought, that the duties of his state and the pleasures of his palace, were equally neglected.

But after awhile his minister returned, having subdued the king's enemies in the hills, and is amazed and disgusted to find his king in close conference with a naked mendicant, instead of occupying himself as formerly with his appointed duties.

He quickly ascertains the pretensions of the ascetic, and asked the king if what he had heard of the mendicant's celestial visit was true.

The king assured him that it was, and the ascetic offered to satisfy the general's apparent scepticism, by departing for Swarga in his presence.

With this intent the king and his courtiers accompanied the Sramanaka to his cell, which he entered, and closed the door.

After some delay, the general asked the king when they would see him again. The king answered, 'Have patience, on these occasions the sage quits his earthly body and assumes an ethereal form in which alone he can enter Indra's heaven.'

' If this be the case,' said the general, ' let

us burn his cell, and thus prevent his re-assuming his earthly body ; your majesty will then have constantly an angelic person in your presence.'

To reconcile the king to this mode of proceeding the general tells him a story which has reference to the serpent, or Nâga tribes of ancient India.

'A Brahman named Devasarman had no child, which denial made his wife miserable. At length, however, owing to some mystic words, a son is promised, but what was the surprise of the mother, and the horror of the attendants, when the child so eagerly desired proved to be a snake.

'The assistants wished to destroy the monster, but maternal affection prevailed, and the snake was reared with all possible care and affection.

'At the proper age the mother entreated her husband to provide a suitable wife for their son. He said he would if he could gain admission to Patâla, where Vasuki, the Serpent King, reigns over the Nâgas, and might grant such a request.

'But his wife was so distressed that to

divert her thoughts he consented to travel.
After some months they arrived at a city in
which a Brahman offered his own beautiful
daughter as a wife for the serpent.

'The girl consented to the marriage and
performed her duties admirably. After a
time her serpent-husband changed one night
into a man, intending in the morning to re-
assume his serpent form : but the girl's father
discovering that the snake body was abandoned, seized the deserted skin and threw it
into the fire.

'The consequence of which was, that his
son-in-law ever remained in the figure of a
man, to the pride of his parents, and the
happiness of his wife.'

After hearing this narrative the king no
longer hesitated. The mendicant's cell was
set on fire; the mendicant perished in the
flames, and the king was as his general
desired, released from the thraldom of a
cunning ascetic.[1]

When Swami was a boy, his youthful
imagination was fired by these ancient Hindu
stories, but the one which tended most

---

[1] From ' Ancient and Mediæval India.'—*Manning.*

directly in forming his ambition, giving him the desire to become a mind-reader, was the following, taken from the 'Vetala-Pancha-vinasati;' or, 'Twenty-five Tales told by a Vetâl.' A Vetâl may be the spirit of a deceased person, or that of a living person who enters the body of another, leaving its own, and taking possession of that of a corpse.

A certain Brahman, named Shantil, gave up the world and lived in the woods as a hermit, or ascetic. He had already become a magician by Yogi-practice. But ordinary magic did not meet his full ambition. He coveted universal superhuman power; and for this he required the co-operation of an able pupil, carefully instructed, who should be qualified to assist in the sacrifice of a specially indicated human being.

Whilst Shantil pursued his ascetic practice, and sat cross-legged, Yogi-fashion, in his forest dwelling, a severe famine occurred in the district of Delhi, or near Hastinapura. The distressed inhabitants dispersed in search of food, and a Brahman, whose wife had died of hunger, wandered with his two sons, who had not yet attained manhood, into what is called a foreign country.

Afar off they perceived a 'forest surrounded by various trees, loaded with ripe fruits; the symmetry, the neatness, and the admirable order of the trees, and the abundance and diversity of a thousand sorts of fruits,' proved most captivating to the hungry men.

Presently they found themselves in front of an edifice, stately as a palace, although built with common materials. Within sat the dreadful magician Shantil.

To the weary wanderers he merely appeared as a holy ascetic; seated on the customary sacred darbha grass, and holding in his hand the usual string of holy beads, which consists of one hundred and eight of the beautifully carved nuts, or seed vessels of the Eleocarpus, here called in Sanskrit Rudrâksha. The travellers approached prostrating themselves, and showing all imaginable reverence.

Shantil returned their salutation, and inquired the object of their journey. Having heard their story he turned to the father and said: 'Oh, Brahman, be not afraid: I will take care of your sons until the famine is over: but on one condition, that you give me one of your boys, whichever you like.'

The father, feeling he had no alternative, consented to the arrangement, and after feasting on dainties for three days, he embraced his sons with many tears, and departed. Shantil was a magician skilled in all arts and sciences: nothing, indeed, was unknown to him.

He lost no time in setting the boys tasks to exercise their faculties, and prepare them also for the acquisition of magic.

He soon ascertained that the younger boy had the higher capacity, and of him he determined to possess himself: he never, therefore, allowed him to go out of his sight. He taught him grammar, divinity, law. astronomy, philosophy, physiognomy, alchemy, geography, the power of transferring the soul to a dead body; the giving it animation, and several other arts, amongst which was included astrology, or the art of foretelling future events. In short, the law which prescribes that a preceptor shall teach all that he knows to his pupil, if he be wise, and desirous of knowledge, was fully obeyed.

In this case, the diligent and accomplished preceptor, was striving to secure an accomplice in a pupil. But, cunning as he was, he out-witted himself; for wishing that the father should prefer the elder lad, he fed him plenti-fully, and clothed him handsomely, whilst he kept his younger and more promising pupil half starved, and poorly clad.

As might be expected, the younger pupil became in consequence anxious to escape, and being already master of the science which prognosticates future events, he perceived that the famine had ceased, and that his father was coming to claim one of his sons and carry him home.

He knew also, that his father would be most attracted by his elder brother, who looked fat, and was covered with jewels. Making use, therefore, of his power of trans-porting himself to distant places, he went to his father, and revealed to him the wicked character and intentions of the Yogin, and obtained a solemn promise that his father would choose him, and not his decorated brother, as the son to be taken home.

The father duly arrived at the hermitage, and though he experienced much difficulty he at length induced the Yogin to part with his gifted pupil, and with him he went away.

But the father and son had not proceeded far before the son felt certain that his tyrant was in pursuit, and for protection he felt it necessary to change himself into a horse. At the same time, he charged his father to sell him at a neighbouring fair ; but for no consideration to part with him to anyone in whose presence he should neigh, or paw the ground.

As the young man apprehended, so it happened. Shantil, the Yogin, tracked them, and discovering the disguise presented himself at the fair, and offered so large a sum that the father, dazzled by the sight of an enormous heap of gold, sold his son to his dreaded enemy.

In vain the poor horse had neighed, over and over, and pawed the ground to show his displeasure at the sale, but this only confirmed Shantil in his desire to have him, so that the money-loving father was prevailed upon to sell him.

Shantil then rides his captive back to his hermitage keeping him under severe restraint : but after a few days the imprisoned horse is able to make himself known to his brother, who loosens his bonds, when he bounds away.

Again Shantil pursues, and again the fugitive escapes. On this occasion assuming the form of a pigeon, he flies in at the open window of the king's palace and is protected and concealed for a time by a lovely princess.

But Shantil was his master in the arts of magic, and every disguise was discovered. Upon his father he could not depend, for his father had sold him for gold. One refuge alone remained ; Shantil had no power over Vetâls—the spirits which animate dead bodies, and despairing of other refuge, the young Brahman Yogin rushed into a corpse which was hanging on a tree in a public cemetery.

This obliged Shantil to seek for a man with sufficient nerve and resolution to go alone to the cemetery at night, cut down the body which contained the Vetâl into which his pupil had entered, and bring corpse and Vetâl to an appointed shrine, at which he would await them.

The man of dauntless courage and resolution was found in King Vikrama. Now, we do not know which Vikrama is meant, he of Ougein, A.D. 65, or Harsha Vikrama, of A.D. 500, but it does not signify, but the city is called Dhara, to the south of the river Godavery.

In Hindu poetry and fiction Vikrama continually figures as the representative of victorious courage. In this work he is described as handsome as the god of love, a devotee in religious worship, deferential to priests, hermits, and persons who disgusted with wordliness and contumely of relatives, had given themselves up to think of God.

He was skilled in sacred sciences ; warlike, though merciful ; a cherisher of the poor, and a comforter of his subjects ; whom he loved as if they were his children.

The palace of King Vikrama was large and magnificent. It contained the most splendid and costly articles : it was constantly sprinkled with aloes water, and every article of furniture was adorned by precious stones.

One day whilst Vikrama sat as usual on his throne, Shantil, the Yogin, presented himself, and so holy did he appear that the king received him with the utmost reverence, and coming down from his throne entreated his guest to take his seat. He then stood with clasped hands and paid him adoration.

Shantil presented an artificial fruit which he had brought, gave the benediction and went away. For several successive days the same thing was repeated, until on one occasion the king happened to drop the fruit which had been presented to him, a pet monkey broke it open, and a splendid ruby was seen within.

Thereupon the king desired to have all the other fruits which the holy man had presented, brought into his presence, and each fruit, when opened was found to contain rubies. The jewels were of the utmost rarity. Indeed, the smallest were of such value, that the largest could only be considered as beyond all price.

'Hermit,' said the king, 'with what intention didst thou present me with such treasures; hast thou anything to ask of me?'

Shantil did not at once acknowledge what it was he wanted, but gradually revealed that he was engaged in rites for obtaining superhuman faculties, and that for their completion he required the personal assistance of the king.

He had travelled over the greater part of the world, he said, vainly seeking such a person as would suit his enterprise. 'At length,' he continued, 'I came to your court. and have found in your Majesty the physiognomy of a person fitted to act as assistant in the intended sacrifice.'

The king did not give him time to say more, but eagerly promised to do whatever was required.

Shantil then explained that a certain Vetâl must be captured and given into his possession.

'On the 14th of Aswin,' said he, 'at midnight, your Majesty must go alone to the cemetery on the banks of the Godavery, beyond the town: you must be clothed in black and bear in your hand a naked sword.'

When the appointed day arrived a certain tree was pointed out from which he was to cut down the required corpse, and having thrown it across his shoulders carry it in perfect silence to Shantil.

Vikrama went and found this burial-ground filled with smoke from burning corpses, and resounding with piercing cries of devils, which were coming from all regions.

At length King Vikrama found the tree, and climbing into it, he cut the cord by which the corpse was suspended and threw it on the ground; but just as he put out his hands to capture the Vetâl it jumped up, and suspended itself as before, high up in the tree.[1]

This happened more than once, until the king discovered that he must bind the corpse across his back before he came down.

And now the king encountered another difficulty; for the wily Vetâl within the corpse which he carried began telling stories, to beguile the fatigue of the journey he said, but in truth, because he wanted to escape; and Vikrama could only hold him on condition of his being absolutely silent.

The Vetâl's plan was therefore, to put the

---

[1] Certain trees are considered the true home of the Vetâl: he is then said ' to live in his own house.'

king off his guard, and just when his interest was excited to ask some pointed question. Five-and-twenty times did this succeed. As soon as the king spoke the Vetâl flew back to his tree, and the whole process had to be repeated. The five-and-twenty stories called 'Vetâlapanchavinsati,' are a record of the tales related on these occasions, which Crustnath Cassinathjee, a modern Hindu, translated recently into English.

What ultimately became of the persecuted Vetâl we will leave to the reader who delights to revel in Eastern fairy lore, as did Swami from his boyhood upwards.

Magic and mystery possessed a charm for him that he could not overcome, the result being that he too desired superhuman power, which should astonish even the advanced scientists of the twenty-first century.

# CHAPTER IX

'I know the wealth of every urn
In which unnumbered rubies burn,
Beneath the pillars of Chilminar;
I know where the isles of perfume are,
Many a fathom down in the sea,
To the south of sun-bright Araby;
I know too, where the Genii hid
The jewelled cup of their King Jamshid,
With life's elixir sparkling high.'

*Lalla Rookh.*

SWAMI being in the possession of all the accumulated knowledge of successive generations of Yogins, and having grown up as it were at the feet of Gamaliel, in the person of his father—to whom had been imparted the secrets of the ascetics of previous generations—was filled with wonderful wisdom.

Moreover, his powers were considerably perfected and strengthened by reason of his advanced culture, aided by his natural gift of psychic-energy; which latter was considerably augmented by the soul-sustaining elixir upon which, it was said, he was chiefly nourished. Rich and poor flocked to him in their emergencies; and it must be recounted of him that although he knew very well that the latter could in no wise adequately reward him, nevertheless, he gave the needy as much of his valuable time as he could well afford; for his rich customers kept him so fully occupied that he had hardly an hour in the day to call his own.

It goes without saying that most of the difficulties upon which he was consulted proceeded from that arch mischief-maker—Jealousy, whose wiles with the human heart have cost mankind no end of trouble, in all ages. It was no uncommon occurrence for a fair Duchess to come and seek his aid by informing her how and where her noble husband was spending his evenings. But the Duke guessing full well that she would be making tender inquiries respecting him, would beforehand endeavour to bribe the high-minded Eastern to keep his tongue from telling.

Or an over-anxious wife would worry herself concerning the safety of her husband who

had taken his monthly journey across the
Atlantic in his flying machine, of which she
was most nervous.

Or a young man striving to obtain a
Government appointment, sought to learn if
his lady friend, of whom he was in mortal
fear, would bowl him out in the coming
examination.

Or an intending disputant in a law case
would consult the all-knowing-one as to the
issue of his suit, if he engaged in it. Those
foolhardy enough to disregard his warnings,
invariably proved unfortunate ; so that in the
end, the great mind-reader got as many of
these clients as the most popular barrister ;
but bearing different results. No matter of
what the difficulty consisted this Anglo-
Eastern sage solved it satisfactorily.

There was a time when the female portion
of his *clientèle* harried him unfairly, by dis-
regarding his professional hours, and coming
to consult him late in the evening. This grew
so distressing to the gentle Eastern that in
the end he made a stand for liberty, by closing
his doors against them at a certain hour. It
was not their desire to harass their favourite

fortune-teller, but they objected to being seen making him their visits; for the raillery of their acquaintances gave these anxious fair ones excruciating agonies.

So Swami commanded his servants to admit no one after nine o'clock; for listening to the recital of his client's case was but a moiety of the labour to be expended over it.

Swami was a man of moderate height, that is to say, moderate for the twenty-first century, when everybody nearly, attained a great stature. His shoulders did not measure the breadth of the Teuton's, nevertheless, he knew no chest-weakness, for his daily athletic exercises from the age of six gave him a constitution that bore the changes of the English climate admirably.

He had the beautifully soft, and peculiarly shaped eyes of his race, that looked dark, dreamy and unfathomable.

His black silken hair hung in natural ringlets around his neck, which was smooth and of a deep cream colour: his complexion was the same, but was relieved by the dark silky moustache which partially concealed his well-cut lips.

His nose was straight, coming in a line almost from the forehead, while his chin was prominent and broad, indicating resolution of character.

The forehead was high and full; while the whole expression of his countenance gave the impression of his being a thinker, rather than a man of action. Although he was averse to much speech nevertheless, his natural fluency of language gave him such choice of words that he always expressed himself with great grace and dignity.

Notwithstanding all his wisdom and deep learning there was such an indescribable air of simplicity and naturalness about him, that people were inspired more with feelings of trust and affection for him, rather than those of awe and wonder.

If you endeavoured to guess his profession by his appearance you might have said he was a poet, philosopher, or scholar, but never a builder, architect, or civil engineer; for in truth, he was a dreamer only, and took no interest in practical pursuits. Nevertheless the nature of his occupation prevented him from spending his time in mere contemplation, where he could live in a world of his own creation; for his mind being daily taken up with the affairs of others, forced him into the outside world, although only in spirit. Seated in his 'room of contemplation,'—as his Eastern servants named it,—where he was surrounded with his books and instruments of magic, and attired in a robe of rich yellow silk that floated down his figure in ample folds, with turban of the same hue, half concealing his dark silky hair, he looked indeed, a perfect picture of Eastern beauty.

He was a bachelor, so that the disturbing influence to the exercise of genius of which our eighteenth-century artist [1] complained, did not interfere with his occupations. The halo that surrounds the unappropriated man had spread its lustre over him, making the pulse of many a maiden quicken beneath the soft glance of those beautiful Eastern eyes of his.

Even the noblest dame would hardly have hesitated to mate with a man who was so universally admired and reverenced. Indeed, rumour averred, that offers of marriage were

---

[1] Sir Joshua Reynolds maintained that a wife and children spoilt an artist's genius.

by no means a rare occurrence with him, for woman's privileges extended to this departure from ancient usage by this time.

But Swami resisted the tender advances of his fair customers, for his life was so entirely devoted to the profession he loved that marital cares had no charm for him.

Moreover, he had never met with the woman who could hold empire over him; whose soul-energy, could mingle with his, and fill his whole being with rapturous emotion, giving his life new charms, new hopes, and new aspirations. Until that being came into his life he was determined to live secluded and solitary, for, making no intimates of his customers, the pleasures of friendship were unknown to him.

One soft spring afternoon a few days, previous to that appointed for the Great Test Tournament, there came rolling up to his residence the royal carriage, drawn by prancing horses, and who should alight therefrom but the Emperor Felicitas himself. The dark servants trembled at the approach of such a mighty potentate, for Eastern ideas of the power of princes are not easily overcome, but Swami himself received the monarch with that easy and gentle courtesy, he extended to everybody.

'What doth the Emperor of so many dominions require of me?' he asked, with a touch of his native Eastern politeness.

'Indeed,' cried the Emperor impetuously, 'I wish my crown anywhere but on my head! What good is power if it leave one craving for that which he most desires?'

'I want that, Swami, which I am denied, and which my heart is bursting for—the love of a woman—there! If thou hast magic power, as I am told thou possessest greatly, tell me how I can attain this?'

'Is she so perverse?' asked Swami quietly.

'Perverse isn't the word for it—she is ice, adamant—immovable as a rock! Yes,' returned the Emperor despondently, 'she is as cold as she is beautiful; and I have put her in prison! And, oh, I am utterly miserable. Believe me, Swami, I cannot sleep, eat, or work, for I am intensely, hopelessly miserable.'

'I am truly sorry to see thy Majesty in such a plight,' remarked Swami kindly. But why didst thou place the lady thou lovest in a prison? It seems a high-handed way of dealing with a subject; truly a mighty strange method of inducing her love?'

'I was put in a quandary,' replied Felicitas candidly, for he knew there was no good gained by attempting to deceive the thought-reader; 'I was suddenly surprised by visitors as I was attempting to detain her, when a craven spirit entered me, and I denounced her as a would-be murderer.'

'Did she endeavour to harm thee?' inquired Swami eagerly.

'Yes, truly she raised her ebony life-preserver to strike me if I touched her.'

'But she did it in self-defence, evidently,' retorted Swami, while a bright light illumined his usually dreamy eyes.

'Besides, those ebony trifles that ladies sometimes carry do not kill, they do but temporarily paralyse the part they touch.'

'Oh, it matters little now, what they do—I wish she had killed me outright—anything but this dreadful torture of doubt to go through. This frightful fear nearly drives me mad—I wish it were all over.'

'What?' inquired Swami, wishful to

obtain a clear command from the king in so many words, for his thoughts were in a state of the wildest confusion.

'The trial—the trial—I dread it. I heartily wish I had never sent that warrant. The Crown Prosecutor has got the case in hand, and, Swami, I am heartily ashamed of it. Help me, I pray thee, and tell me how it will all end, and I will well reward thee.'

The Emperor looked like one distraught; his blue eyes gleamed with feverish excitement: his lips twitched uneasily, and he clasped his hands together with the agony of his mind, over which fear more than repentance predominated.

Swami soon perceived wherein the Emperor's chief trouble lay. 'I see by the brain-waves emanating from thee that the woman thou lovest is in confinement in the first-class misdemeanants' quarters, in the Metropolitan Prison. Now that will do; I know enough. Let thy Majesty come at this hour to-morrow, and I will show thee what thou desirest to learn.'

Then the Emperor remembering that the real object of his visit was not yet accomplished, blurted out—'I desire to learn the issue of the trial, that is my chief care at present.'

'Of that I am aware, Sire,' replied Swami courteously. 'Thou desirest to learn the issue of the trial on thine own account. I perfectly understand it. In the meantime I would advise that the lady be allowed her liberty, subject to her own recognisances. It will be more advisable from every point of view, lest thy subjects deem thee harsh and unjust towards her. Whichever way the trial goes it is wise to show a merciful bearing, so that thou mayest retain thy subjects' good opinion. It cannot hurt the case for the lady will not flee, be well assured of that. She will prefer to face her case in open court, for by all accounts that have reached me of her character, Mercia isn't made of stuff to shirk a duty.'

'Ha, Sorcerer, thou knowest her name! Who told it thee?' exclaimed Felicitas in much surprise.

'Thyself,' replied the Soul-Reader, 'I read it on thy brain. Moreover, fear, more than love, predominates within thy bosom. Thy

Majesty doth dread the testimony of the witnesses arrayed against thee.'

'I do not deny it,' returned Felicitas meekly, for he was completely subdued by the two-fold influence of anxiety concerning the impending case, and awe of the Soul-reader's power to divine his thought.

'I do not indeed, deny it,' he continued, ' for I certainly dread that awful Sadbag, who with villainous guile hid behind the screen, and heard me plead my cause with the beauteous Mercia. But I must own it gives me more uneasiness the testimony of Mercia herself, for none will doubt her word.'

' Then, let me advise thy Majesty to withdraw the charge and set the lady at liberty forthwith. A king's cause should be just, and beyond suspicion : himself the personification of integrity, truth, and righteousness. He should rather suffer a slight, than in revenge work a great injury. The way of a king should be perfect.'

Felicitas looking ill at ease endeavoured to take this rebuke lightly. ' The law still holds good that " a king can do no wrong." But, Swami,' he continued earnestly, and in a pleading tone, 'thine advice is good if my way be not : tell me first what the issue of the trial will be, and I will then accommodate myself to circumstances.'

'Be it so,' answered Swami courteously. 'Come at this hour to-morrow and I will be prepared.'

When the Emperor arrived on the following day at the Soul-reader's dwelling, he was met at the door by Swami himself, who conducted him into his library. From thence he led him into an inner room, which having no window was in a state of complete darkness.

'It has cost me many hours of labour to obtain this result,' explained Swami to his visitor, 'but it is, I believe, perfect. Presently, I will illumine the sensitive plate on which the scene is projected from my brain, and show to thy Majesty three pictures of the scenes which will certainly be enacted at the court, during the coming trial. For I find that the case will come off independently of thy action. I can only now advise what course thy Majesty can best take concerning it.'

Then Swami, having all the results in readiness of his wonderful instrument—the psycho-register—touched a spring, and forthwith an immense illuminated picture, filling one side of the room and representing a scene in the Great Hall, of the Court, almost dazzling in its brilliancy of colouring, instantaneously appeared. So complete was the surprise of Felicitas that he started back, for the strange vividness, no less than the suddenness of the scene made him somewhat nervous: but Swami, accustomed to finding his visitors startled, kindly re-assured him.

' Sire,' said he gently, ' be not alarmed, there is nothing to hurt thy Majesty.'

It proved, in truth, a most wonderful and striking picture of the Great Justice Hall in the Metropolitan Court. Tiers of seats containing the *élite* of Great Britain, and Ireland, Berlin, Paris, and most of the European Continent, were filled to overflowing ; for nobles and great dames, and even several crowned heads, had assembled from all parts to see the *cause célèbre*.

In the dock was seated Mercia, looking calm, beautiful, and self-possessed. She was arrayed in a flowing crimson velvet gown that cast a warm glow over her face which had paled considerably either through anxiety, or prison confinement.

Innumerable opera glasses were being levelled at her by both sexes; while busy barristers in their black gowns and white wigs scanned their note-books. The place set apart for newspaper reporters was filled with representatives of the press setting in order their respective phonographs, which were to register the whole proceedings of the case. Where the distance was not great as soon as the court closed each day, the phonograph containing the evidence of the witnesses, speeches of the barristers, and in fact everything that was said at the trial, was packed off forthwith to the editor of each newspaper, by the quickest conveyance possible, who cut down the report as he thought fit, to suit the dimensions of his space in the newspaper, and the fastidiousness of his readers; for the frailties of human nature as delineated in a court of justice do not form at all times an edifying spectacle for the young, or the modest.

On his feet stood the Crown Prosecutor, evidently stating his case, while Geometrus and Sadbag were seated at one side; but no Emperor Felicitas could be discovered anywhere: he indeed, was conspicuous by his absence, seeing he was the only witness in his own case.

Felicitas gazed in amazement at the immense group photographed there; ejaculating from time to time, as he recognised each member of the nobility with whom he was acquainted, pictured before him.

' By Jove!' he exclaimed, ' there is Nicholas of Russia, and his fat Empress! How interested she looks—see she has got her ear-trumpet in use, endeavouring to miss nothing. And Louis of France, forsooth; the new Louis Twentieth, not at all a bad looking fellow! And Osbert my cousin, who averred he'd be dumb, but evidently intends to be neither blind, nor deaf.

' And there's the Duke of Northumberland, with his skinny spouse seated beside him; whose skin is just like a piece of crinkled yellow leather. And Lord Lennox and his pretty bride! Well, I must say, they're all most excellent likenesses—they look indeed, like living pictures. What a treat they are getting! An Emperor in a witness-box isn't an every-day occurrence, to be sure! And, oh, there's Mercia, how pale, how beautiful, how sad she appears! Ah, Swami, I have no heart to go on with this prosecution. I love her—I would die for her—canst thou not exercise thy magic and *make* her love *me?*'

'I possess no power over the human heart,' returned Swami coldly. 'My work is to make known futurity to a slight extent; which will serve as a guidance to the inquirer in matters of difficulty. Besides,' added the Thought-reader lightly, 'thy Majesty is no longer in the matrimonial market. Why trouble then the lady when thou hast nothing to offer her but disgrace?' he inquired after a pause.

'I would make her mine Empress,' cried Felicitas passionately. 'I would obtain a divorce and free myself from my intolerable fetters!'

'Impossible!' urged Swami, as it seemed defiantly. 'Thy Majesty hath no just cause for putting away thine Empress : she is a model of marital purity, by all accounts.'

'My plea would be on the ground of incompatibility of temper : we do not agree in any way, and I shall never know happiness while I live with her. Besides, what is to become of the Succession, with a barren woman for Empress?' demanded Felicitas with a look of triumph in his face, for he imagined this would prove an unanswerable argument with the country.

'The Succession,' returned Swami smiling, ' can take no harm whatever, with the numerous cousins thy Majesty is favoured with. Moreover, it behoves me to remind thy Majesty that the Empress and thyself lived in perfect harmony up to the time that thy mind wandered to the fair astronomer. Curb thy desires : keep thy way pure, and engage thyself in the affairs of the nation, taking good heed of thine high position, and Mercia will soon pass out of thy life. Thus all will in time go well with thee.'

'How fine thou preachest, good Swami ! Surely thou hast mistaken thy vocation— for the gown of a priest would better befit thee.  Dost thou advise all thy customers in this strain?' exclaimed the monarch angrily.

'I counsel each one who seeks my aid to the best of my ability.  All who come hither do so of their own free will.  I invite no one —I press no one.  Let him who is dissatisfied with my forewarnings go his own way: I. will not quarrel with him for following his own council.  For I find all men in the end carry out their own designs, even if the wisdom of a Solomon, double-distilled, were to warn them of their folly.'

'Swami, forgive me!' returned Felicitas humbly, 'I meant no offence; but I was nettled by being made to listen to good advice, to which I am treated daily.  The Empress bestows uninvited this article so generously that in truth I want no more from anybody.  Now, I pray, let us talk of Mercia; would she marry me if I were free?'

'She is destined for another, far beneath thy Majesty in social position; but who can give her a heart wholly devoted to her: one who has never desired the love of woman till his eyes gazed upon her beauty—the beauty of her soul,' replied Swami, with a countenance irradiated with his own emotions.

'To look at thee, Swami, and to hear thy speech,' cried the Emperor excitedly, 'one could only conclude that thou wert in love with her thyself! Her beauty of person is good enough for me: I know naught of soul-beauty! Few men do, I opine, save sorcerers; and they need no femininities to comfort them, being above such frailties, I presume. However, I am aware that Mercia is in love already. That fellow Geometrus desires her, and she loves him: at all events she told me as much. I suppose thy prophecy refers to him; for he is one also who troubles little about the affairs of women; for he slaves all day making astronomical instruments for Mercia to do her star-gazing with. He is her devoted servant, and she appreciates him accordingly,' observed Felicitas cynically.

'But will she *marry* him?' remarked Swami musingly.

'Exercise thy soul-reading powers and discover for thyself,' answered the Emperor lightly. 'Turn on the next scene, if it be

ready, for I would learn all with as great a
speed as possible,' he added.

Upon hearing this request Swami pressed
another button, and immediately the room
was enveloped in darkness, and the picture
vanished altogether from sight. The next
picture which appeared upon the crystal
plate, portrayed the court with the same
visitors in similar order as before, but with
this difference. The serious expression which
the countenances of all present wore in the
first instance was now changed to that of
intense excitement in some, while the greater
part of the audience seemed bursting with
merriment.

Sadbag, who was the centre of all eyes,
was in the witness-box manipulating a phonograph of the newest design, the boxed-up
talk of which was being apparently reeled
out for the benefit of the court; the nature
of its revelations proving irresistibly comic to
the assembly's point of view, while the old
man's air of triumph most graphically seemed
to · say, 'What do you think of that my
friends?' as he smirked with an 'I-told-you-
so,' sort of expression on his face.

Mercia on her part was blushing violently, Geometrus was scowling darkly, while all the barristers were endeavouring to conceal their merriment by fluttering their pocket-handkerchiefs under the pretence of blowing their noses. Prince Osbert was actually holding his sides; while his face, puckered with merriment, seemed to say—'Now isn't this excruciatingly funny?'

Mercia's counsel wore an air of happy triumph, which appeared to indicate complete satisfaction with his own good management of the case. Felicitas was absent, as before, but his Empress was among the audience, looking as flushed and angered as an injured wife might well be.

'What the deuce is everybody laughing at?' queried the Emperor, while a deep frown crossed his face,—'I cannot understand it!'

Swami remained silent; he knew full well what the phonograph was saying, but did not deem it wise to give the irascible monarch too much information.

'Canst not thy Majesty comprehend the situation?' he demanded suavely.

'No, I do not,' answered Felicitas hotly. ' tell me the meaning of it all.'

'Time alone will show the full development. There is sufficient pictured to give thy Majesty ample warning.'

'It is easy enough to see that I shall be made a pretty laughing-stock for the whole world. That villain Sadbag has worked some vile trick upon me—that is very evident. Strange that thou art unable to explain what the beast is up to!' muttered Felicitas to himself, for he was bursting with rage at the very thought of the whole proceeding.

'We have had enough of this,' observed Swami quietly, as he prudently pressed the extinguishing button, producing perfect darkness. 'We will now show the closing scene and dismiss the matter for to-night.'

'I am weary of it all,' remarked the monarch disgusted with the portrayals of the magic crystal, 'I would I had never seen this sorcery, I shall not get a wink of sleep this night.'

'Nor to-morrow night either,' said Swami coolly, as he switched on the light revealing the third and last of the wonderful pictures.

'What meanest thou by that?' inquired Felicitas curtly.

'The real trial commences to-morrow,' replied the Soul-reader calmly, 'a messenger is at this moment awaiting thy Majesty's return to remind thee of the date.'

'To-morrow!' repeated the Emperor, 'impossible! This cannot be the date!'

'It is truly,' said Swami compassionately, 'thine hour of trial is at hand. But see, here is Mercia's hour of triumph, mark how everybody is showing her honour, and offering their congratulations.'

However striking these photo-crystal pictures had appeared, this last, without doubt, displayed the most stirring scene. It represented the intense joy of a great multitude. who were offering their congratulations, and testifying their admiration of one who had gone through a severe ordeal, out of which she had come victorious.

The whole populace were paying her their sincerest homage in honest English fashion. Some were waving their hats and cheering vociferously. While a number had removed from their shafts the four bay horses that drew her chariot.  This latter was standing near the gates of the law courts, and the men in warm enthusiasm, had commenced pulling the carriage themselves.

Others were casting wreaths of bay leaves into her lap; so numerous were they that a great pile was being formed in the centre of her carriage.  These were intermixed with bouquets of the loveliest flowers, one of which was composed of the most cunningly-wrought blossoms, the leaves of which were studded with costly emeralds, and their buds bedewed with diamonds of immense value.  This beautiful and generous gift was being offered by a gentleman whose face being turned aside, made the Emperor unable to discover the features.

Mercia looked perfectly radiant with pleasure, as she bowed her numerous acknow-ledgments to the enthusiastic crowd that sur-rounded her.

'By Jove!' exclaimed the Emperor ex-citedly, as he critically scanned the mysterious figure, 'I could swear those were thy dark curls clustering round thine ears!'

'Curls are common enough, Sire, and dark

hair is no rarity in thy realms,' replied Swami evasively, who seemed a little put out at the king's speech.

Felicitas gazed with feelings of wonder and envy, intermingled with regret, upon the picture which glowed with resplendent colouring; every figure in which presented such an apparent natural roundness that it was difficult to imagine they were not endowed with life and motion. The lineaments of those with whom he was acquainted were so exactly delineated, and the natural pose and bearing of each individual so vividly represented that he was impelled to put out his hand to touch one of them.

'Hold!' exclaimed Swami quickly, 'touch it not, or thou art a dead man! The shock would kill thee instantly, for these psycho-developments are wrought and illumined by strong frictional electricity of the deadliest kind; the current of which is so powerful that it infinitely exceeds that of forked lightning.'

'Ha!' ejaculated Felicitas paling, 'it is certainly foolhardy to meddle with such trickery; but, in truth, I had forgotten myself completely. It is without doubt the most beautiful creation I have ever seen! How wonderfully art thou endowed, Swami, I would I were only half as gifted as thou art.' Then, the Emperor fixing his gaze upon the beauteous face of Mercia, who formed the central figure in the scene, and whose countenance expressed the sweetest grace and modesty; commenced to thus apostrophise her—'This then is the end and issue of my suit——'

'Which suit, thy lovesuit, or thy lawsuit?' interrupted Swami lightly; for the Emperor's love-raptures for some reason annoyed him.

'Which suit?' repeated Felicitas dreamily.

'Both suits, I suppose,' added Swami laughingly.

'Ah truly,' sighed the Emperor, ' the twain have proved an utter failure. I thought to bring her low—to humiliate her—to place her in such a position as would force her to accept my royal clemency and bounty; but alas, I have only brought about a public triumph for her, and public dishonour to myself! Oh, Swami let not this be the finishing scene; thou art all-powerful, make another wherein Mercia is my bride, the crowned Empress of the Teutonic Empire.'

' Be it so, Sire, a fourth picture shall appear wherein the completion of her triumph shall be projected. Retire a few moments, and I will conjure it presently.'

In less than ten minutes, Felicitas was summoned into the dark room, and on the wonderful crystal there appeared the most beautiful vision of womanly loveliness that art had ever created. Mercia looking radiant with happiness, whose beauty was heightened and enhanced by the most costly draperies and diamonds that wealth could produce, was seated on a throne, surrounded by the imposing pageantry of a coronation ceremony. A crown composed of magnificent diamonds and various precious stones of immense value graced her well-shaped head, while brilliant gems sparkled in the rich embroidery of her magnificent robes.

Eastern potentates, and native princes of the various Eastern possessions were paying her homage. Their Oriental costumes, rich with jewels and resplendent with vivid colouring lent a charm to the most magnificent scene of Oriental splendour that it was possible to conceive.

'What an entrancing sight! What perfect loveliness!' murmured the Emperor, as he gazed with rapture on the beautiful picture before him.

'Mercia, dearest Mercia, how beautiful thou art! Did I not divine thou wert made to grace a throne? Oh, thou sweet Mercia, listen to me. What bliss to dwell with thee always; to listen to the divine melody of that sweet voice; to clasp in mine that beautiful hand; to drink of the nectar of those ruby lips; to know that thou wert all mine own!

'Oh, that I might share my crown, my realms, my all with thee! Thou Queen of my heart, thou Light of my life!

'Art thou indeed to grace my throne? Is this thy Bridal Day foreshown? Swami,' continued he, turning to the Soul-reader, 'is all that Eastern pageantry to lend its lustre to my second nuptials?'

'Surely not,' answered Swami proudly, 'does not thy Majesty perceive that it is altogether an Oriental picture?'

'But I am the Emperor of India,' said

Felicitas with much dignity, 'how then can Mercia be Empress unless *I* place the consort crown on her head?'

'The days are numbered that see thee supreme Ruler of my country : a week hence and India will have accomplished her freedom.'

'Has fate decreed that the Hindu shall exceed the English in physical strength? If this be thy divination then I believe nothing of it.'

' All the worse for thee, Sire. Believe that which yields thee most comfort, and forget my harmless prophecies. To-morrow attend the Law Courts, and see all things reversed, as thy heart desireth. Perhaps, like dreams, which are said to prove the contrary of what they picture, the reality will come out the opposite of all thou hast seen this day portrayed. It may be that Mercia, instead of being crowned an Empress, shall to-morrow be consigned to execution, or life imprisonment?'

'I would sooner see her die than wedded to another,' murmured the Emperor moodily.

'Thy Majesty is merciful as wise!' re-

sponded Swami cynically, as he pressed the
extinguisher for the last time, and set the
room in darkness ; obliterating for the moment
the entrancing portrait of the woman he was
learning to love through the medium of soul-
sympathy ; for he was as yet personally unacquainted with Mercia.

'I would I had never seen either thyself
or thy psychical pictures,' said Felicitas bitterly. 'What good is it looking into futurity ?
It does but make one miserable beforehand.
I cannot control the current of events ; all
will take place exactly the same as if I had
known nothing. To look into the future is
but to anticipate life's troubles.

'What earthly use to learn the issue of
the trial to day, to-morrow would have been
soon enough to know my ill-fortune.'

'Balak-like thou wouldst have me curse,
when I can only bless,' returned Swami. 'It
is true that thy Majesty must reap as thou
hast sown. We all live under this unalterable
law. As the husbandman sows seed expecting
its like to be reproduced, so we must be satisfied to gather the fruit of our own actions.
If we plant the crab, can we look for the

apricot?  If we work dishonourable actions, can we reap honour thereby?

'The priest promises Heaven as the reward of a good life, but the only Heaven assigned to man is that of his own creation—the delight that pervades his soul in the knowledge that he has not lived in vain ; that he has been the source of comfort and happiness to others ; that he has kept the golden rule.  Six little words, in fact, define it,—*that he loves and is beloved*—for human love, in all its various sections, is Heaven—no other Paradise exists.'

' 'Tis the want of this, that's brought my trouble,' murmured Felicitas.  'If I had Mercia's love then wouldst thou see how pious I could be.'

'Is a child contented wholly when one desire is satisfied?  No, he cries hourly for new toys and new delights.  Thy Majesty would weary in course of time with the beauteous Mercia, as thou hast wearied of thy spouse.  Physical charms delight the eye for a season ; but if there be no union of psycho-magnetic sympathy there is no possibility of an enduring affection.  Sire, be content ; as thou hast made thy bed, so must thou lie upon it.'

'That reminds me of my suit to-morrow,' interrupted Felicitas impatiently. 'What wouldst thou advise in this dilemma?'

'The case is surrounded with difficulties,' answered Swami reflectively. 'If thou withdraw the prosecution, the defenders would persist in its being gone through. Sadbag, and Mercia's counsel would not miss giving the evidence they have in store, under any consideration. Her counsel has decidedly made up his mind that nothing shall induce him to let the case collapse. He will plead, if thou withdraw, that his client's character is at stake, and must be cleared by suitable investigation of the charge. Besides, the charge is *thine* no longer: it is in the hands of the Public Prosecutor.'

'I will be no witness for him,' cried Felicitas, a new idea having crossed his mind. 'This night urgent affairs of state shall summon me to Berlin. Good-bye, Swami, for the present. We shall see whether thy soul-reading crystal plate has discovered to us the false or the true.'

'Will thy Majesty be absent from the GREAT TEST TRIAL next Tuesday?' inquired

Swami, with a view of reminding him of the date of that event.'

' By all above us, no,' emphatically ejaculated Felicitas, whose ideas and recollections were in a decided jumble. The Emperor, if he be alive, must without doubt, be present at the Tournament.

'I do not see how it could legally take place without me; for the king, whose realms are in dispute, is ever deemed the chiefest witness of the contest.

'I have ample time; for by to-morrow night Mercia's cause will have been heard and fully disposed of; there are still a few days left for the scandal to blow over, before the 1st of May, when I will appear in my proper place, and fulfil the duties that belong to my royal state.'

' How convenient to be a king, and know naught of the penalties of wrong-doing. A meaner mortal would be punished for perjury in such a case! But here 'twill be glossed over, and the Emperor's clemency enlarged upon by his counsel,' thought Swami, as he conducted the monarch to the great doors, outside which his carriage stood in readiness.

# CHAPTER X

' Whence all this strange attraction ?   'Tis Nature's law,
Which irresistibly impels and leads
With forces so unutterably strong,
And yet so hid—so wrapped in joy—concealed—
That whence it comes we nothing know, nor why—
We only know it is that Power called LOVE.'
*Idylls, Legends and Lyrics.*

As soon as Swami got rid of his visitor, he quickly made his way to the dark chamber, where he had been thirsting to rush for some time past, and turning on the force brought to view the psycho-development of the coronation scene, wherein the portrait of the beautiful astronomer was the centre-piece. He had in reality prepared this mental feast for himself, but was induced at the request of Felicitas to reveal its charms to that monarch.

As she sat upon her golden throne surrounded by the Maharajahs, and Heads of the various Principalities of the Eastern Empire, decked in their glittering robes, their crowns,

and other courtly splendours, heightened
with all the attendant pomp of Eastern cere-
monial, Swami saw only the person of the
matchless Mercia; for the rest possessed little
interest for him at this moment.

As his gaze dwelt upon her sweet face, he
looked into her eyes with rapturous emotion,
and clasping his hands together, knelt before
this lovely delineation of his secret adoration,
uttering in tenderest accents a passionate
apostrophe.

' O, divine Mercia, I love thee! Thou hast
brought into my life a new element—a new
force, as mysterious, as it is powerful. A
new joy has come into my heart hitherto
unknown. A new hope is imparted to my
lonely life, irradiating its darkness, and giving
the sweetest comfort known to the human soul.
I read the magic mirror of thine eyes, and
see thy soul all perfect, all pure, and unsullied.

' I mentally see thy thought, and mapped
out before me read the loveliness of thy mind;
for by the motions of thy brain I am acquainted
with the rich treasures of thy cultured mind.

' Thou wert made to inspire the deepest
emotions in the human heart; for the mighty

gift of soul-sympathy that pervades thy whole being, exercises such power over every mind that all bow to thy magic influence, deeming it a happiness to be near thee, however short the moment.

'The lowliest feel thy charm, and draw comfort therefrom, while I, dearest Mercia, am inspired with ineffable delight; for who could know thee and not be fired with the noblest aims—the highest aspirations?

'Come then, sweet girl, come hither, and let mine eyes gaze upon the casket that contains such a rich jewel—the form that contains such a perfect soul!'

Then Swami, raising himself from his kneeling posture, and standing erect, closed his eyes, and projecting from his nerve-centres a powerful stream of psychic-energy, which, rushing in waves through the air, almost instantly found its way to the fair prisoner.

Immediately, without knowing the cause, she commenced thinking of the great Soul-reader, experiencing a strong desire to go and see him.

Now, in consequence of Swami's advice the day previous, the Emperor had, at the proper quarters intimated his desire to bestow the royal pardon on the fair culprit; which command being as quickly carried out as officialism would admit, Mercia was made acquainted with her position with little delay.

When the governor of the prison read the document to Mercia which contained the so-called 'pardon,' an indignant flush rose instantly to her cheeks.

' Ah ! ' she disdainfully cried, ' the Emperor generously sends me a pardon before it is solicited, for a crime I have never committed ! His clemency oppresses me—it is really more than I can accept.'

' It is certainly most unparalleled in prison records,' remarked the governor, who looked mystified. ' I don't know of a similar instance in all my experience. The pardon should be accorded after the sentence is passed, should the prisoner be found guilty. I understand that his Gracious Majesty being himself the prosecutor, departs from the ordinary routine observed in such matters. He desires to set thee at liberty without further delay.'

' I cannot accept his Majesty's clemency without consulting my counsel,' replied Mercia after a pause: 'the case is in readiness, he informs me, and witnesses are fully prepared to establish my innocence. I will therefore remain here until I have had a consultation with him. Be good enough to send for him at once, and we two will consider the matter.'

While the governor of the prison was despatching his messenger to the barrister, Swami's brain-wave had in the meantime reached Mercia; causing her to upset her plans somewhat; for she found herself being impelled by a strong desire to regain her freedom without delay.

Intimating her change of design to the governor, she took her departure from the prison; and hiring a cab from the nearest public stand,—for electricity did not do away with the Jehu, it only altered the motive-power of his chariot—she instinctively gave orders to drive to the great Soul-reader, and ere long found herself at his door.

'Why have I come hither?' she asked herself, as she was being led through the beautiful conservatory, which was brilliantly illumined by electricity, for the sun had gone down by this time.

'What has brought me here?' she murmured again to herself.

'What brings everybody hither?' whispered Reason in her ear.

'Yes, yes,' she replied mentally to her prompter, 'of course I have come to consult the great man in my difficulty. I seek his advice and forewarning concerning the course I ought to pursue to-morrow. This is a great emergency. No barrister can determine how the trial will end; for Justice hath so many ways of turning that the most righteous cause runs great risks in a law court. My case is not an ordinary one; my counsel has had no experience in opposing the suit of an Emperor, for his own Sovereign is his opponent! The whole thing bristles with difficulties throughout.'

A few seconds sufficed for these reflections, for the motions of the brain are intensely rapid: she had only proceeded a few steps when Swami, who had come out to meet her, greeted her with the most profound respect.

His whole deportment displayed the deepest reverence of her, while his countenance was irradiated with the light of a great joy.

'Welcome, sweet Lady!' he murmured softly, 'wilt thou graciously come hither?' Saying which he conducted her into his library, displaying the utmost deference towards her, the while; then leading her to the softest couch he begged her to be seated.

'Thou art Dayanand Swami, the great Soul-reader, and I am Mercia Montgomery, the late Astronomer Royal,' she faltered out, hardly knowing what to say, she felt so singularly disturbed in her mind.

'I have heard great accounts of thine attainments,' replied Swami, endeavouring to check his excitement, 'I have long desired the opportunity of meeting with England's rarest lady.'

Mercia looked at him earnestly for a moment; then blushed, and an instant later recovering herself, she smiled archly—

'Ah!' she exclaimed, 'it seems to me that all men are given to flattery, I imagined that the illustrious Swami would have been an exception.'

'Because all men say the same that proves it is no flattery,' said Swami deprecatingly; 'nevertheless it is not meet that one should give expression to his opinion while yet he is a stranger. Pardon me, Mistress Mercia, for the liberty taken. But let me entreat of thee to raise thy veil; otherwise I shall be at a disadvantage when reading thy destiny, which I presume, is the object of thy visit,' he added artfully.

'Certainly,' answered Mercia innocently; while another bright smile lit up her face with a singular radiance, as she threw back the dark veil with which she had been careful to conceal herself while coming from the prison. 'I do not use these things always,' she added, 'it was the disgrace of being seen come out of a prison that induced me to wear it at all.'

'The disgrace is his who sent thither the innocent. The noon of another day shall place the dishonour where it is due. Lady, I am acquainted with thy design in coming here, it is to learn the issue of thy trial. Rest assured, all is well; the arrangements are perfect that thy friends have made.'

'Even so my counsel tells me: he says the evidence of Sadbag who was in the room during the time that the Emperor accuses me of attempting his life is most convincing. Nevertheless, as the old man himself is accused of conspiring with me against his Majesty, the Emperor, I have my fears anent the trial's issue; for such evidence will not be credited the same as if he were an independent witness. But now the matter has taken another aspect. This day a pardon has come, unsolicited by me, from the Emperor, and I am fully released without a trial, without condemnation, I am *pardoned!* Unfold to me this mystery, I pray, and give me thy good counsel.'

All this time the Soul-reader was gazing upon the beautiful face turned towards him in anxious appeal: knowing full well of the certainty of her position, his mind was not disturbed with the perplexities of the situation. Nevertheless, he deemed it impolitic to explain everything fully: such information could not turn the current of affairs, he argued to himself; it would only have the effect of increasing her reluctance to appear in court at all.

'Let thine anxieties be dispersed at once,' he urged gently, 'there is no cause at all for alarm: only trust thy good friend Sadbag; he will make it pretty warm for the Emperor.'

'How so?' inquired Mercia, with great curiosity.

'By his evidence, of course,' replied Swami, who hesitated to recount the full extent of Sadbag's revelations, which could only increase her embarrassment.

'Is this all then, that the great Soul-reader can show me?' exclaimed Mercia in a disappointed tone of voice; 'I hoped to have seen the wonderful mind-reflecting mirror that all the world speaks of. Is there nothing at all in my future that is worthy of transmission to the plate? If nothing better, then show me my future husband;' she demanded, while a roguish smile dimpled her face.

'Show thee thy future husband!' repeated Swami nervously, 'I cannot, because I dare not,' he added in evident excitement.

'But I desire it,' persisted Mercia, 'I fain would learn if there be such an individual in store for me.'

'I will tell thee whom thou shalt not marry, if that will suit,' returned Swami earnestly; with a view of evading the inquiry.

'That is indeed a negative method of satisfying a lady's curiosity,' laughed Mercia gaily. 'Well, then whom shall I *not* marry?'

'Neither Felicitas, nor Geometrus,' replied he emphatically.

Mercia coloured violently upon hearing Geometrus' name thus mentioned, then trying to regard it lightly, she observed—'Who is it, show me his reflection?'

'Not to-night. Come again, dear lady, and the portrait shall be in readiness for thee.'

'Ah, Swami,' returned Mercia sweetly; 'I perceive that thou art only playing with me. Thou knowest full well, that neither love nor marriage is for me. If I win my case, I return to my post. My work is my bridegroom; I am bound to no other; for therein is centred my every thought—my whole life-work.'

'The observation of the heavenly bodies shall be thy life-work no longer; thou art called to do work even more glorious than the study of the great universe; for thou art destined to rule millions of human beings, whose happiness depends upon thy wisdom, whose well-being is assured by thy just administration. Princes shall pay thee homage: the great ones of the earth shall be proud of thy friendship. All nations shall vie with each other in showing thee honour; and thine own people shall love and adore thee.'

The Soul-reader uttered his prophecy as one in a dream. With his hands clasped together, and quivering with the violence of his emotion, he seemed insensible to his surroundings. His great dark eyes were filled with a wonderful light, whose luminous rays seemed to possess the power of reaching into futurity. Unconsciously to himself, the waves of soul-sympathy filled the air, and entering Mercia's system set her heart beating wildly with an ecstatic pleasure, that was an entirely new experience.

Trembling with delight she awaited the moment when the fever of his excitement should have subsided; and searched his countenance for the first sign, that she might question him further.

' Oh, Swami,' she exclaimed, at length;

for she could wait no longer—'whose kingdom shall I govern, and where are my dominions? Is it well that one so ignorant of State affairs as I should be advanced to such immense responsibility—such power—such glory? Thou hast indeed painted a picture glowing with bright colour. Should not thy psychic power point to some experienced potentate, more worthy than I? Is not this a word-blunder—some curious coincidence of name that hath upset thy calculations? It is not I, Mercia, the astronomer, who is destined for this brilliant future; this most glorious career?'

'It is thou, Mercia, and no other,' responded Swami impressively—'there is no king, or high potentate better fitted for this proud position. If thou art filled with doubts, see the proof, and banish thy scepticism forthwith. Come hither, and look upon thy portrait, brain-painted upon the sensitive plate beneath the crystal.'

Taking her hand he led her, all quivering with emotion, into the dark chamber, when turning on the energy he displayed the glittering picture, ablaze with brilliant colouring;

every figure presenting that aspect of roundness, which seemed to endow it almost with life.

'Oh! It is myself—my very self!' she exclaimed excitedly, her face lit up with the intensity of her varying sensations. 'How beautiful! Is it possible that I shall ever look like that? What splendid jewelled robes! What a magnificent crown, all ablaze with costly diamonds, sapphires, emeralds, and rubies! How rich the Indian gold appears of which the throne is composed, set in contrast with the white marble of the floor!

'What a glorious assemblage of Eastern princes, paying homage to their Empress, and arrayed in all their courtly splendour! This is, truly, a scene from some ancient Eastern fairy tale, told thousands of years ago by the imaginative Asiatic, and thou, Swami, hast made my portrait its centrepiece. Is it not so?' she inquired; for her inherent modesty made her doubt again.

Then, Swami, his dark, speaking eyes filling with tears, and his heart swelling with deep disappointment at seeing her doubt his integrity, for a moment turned upon her a sad, reproachful gaze; when immediately, a sudden passion seized him, forcing him prematurely, and against his judgment, to give it utterance.

'Mercia, dost thou doubt me? Would I deceive the one being for whom my heart yearns? I love thee—I love thee, thou gifted one! Thou art, indeed, soul of my soul, life of my life! Thou art the true living elixir; the true soul-energy which can for all time support my spirit. Thou dost inspire a new energy into my being—a new goal for my aspirations! Thy life-essence can alone mingle with mine, for only thy soul can hold communion with mine.

'Physically, I have never before seen thee. These material, and natural mirrors of the human brain have never until now reflected thine image on their surface; nevertheless, I have gazed on thee through the medium of my soul-sight, and have drank in the delight of thy beauty.

'I have looked into thy very soul, and read its inmost workings—thy beautiful unsullied soul, clear as the limpid waters.

'Thy thought is no longer thine own; it is

MINE, by the gift of DIVINE LOVE! Yea, thou art mine, and I am thine!' Swami gave utterance to his passionate ecstasy as one in a dream, where the faculties being highly exalted create sensations of the most delightful character.

His face, beautiful in feature, and spiritual in expression at all times, was now irradiated with the glowing fire of love.

This new emotion filled him with a subtle rapture, imparting to him a new fervour that lent a charm to every look and motion.

His dreamy eyes had turned intensely brilliant, their excitement spreading to every muscle of the face, imparted over all his countenance a delicious softness, that instantly set every nerve in Mercia's frame a-throbbing.

To her, as to him, it was indeed, a supreme moment, making her dumb by reason of its intensity, as of its suddeness and power. Her countenance was overspread with the warm glow of the unseen, mystic force, while her bosom heaved with tumultuous emotions. Speechless she sat, with downcast eyes, lost in a silent joy, while delicious sensations that were entirely new to her, thrilled her whole frame.

'Is this then LOVE!' she exclaimed at length; while a tone of ineffable tenderness pervaded her utterance, making her voice low, soft, and melodious.

'Am I then too, a victim to this conqueror of the world—a prisoner bound in sweet captivity, with not the faintest wish to cast away my fetters? Is this that strange and subtle power that guides and shapes the destinies of the whole world; whose dominion the strongest bow to, whose sceptre sways over prince and peasant?'

'Even so, sweet Mercia, this is love. This is that which the Gods gave to sweeten the labours of mankind: for who could bear the burden of life from birth to death without this gracious comfort to sustain him?' answered Swami, as moving nearer to her side he took her hand in his, and covered it with passionate kisses.

'I had thought,' she murmured in a low voice ' that love was not for me; that my life should be devoted to my work. That the honour attained by the close fulfilment of my duties would be ample reward.

'My ambition was to endeavour to be the

best astronomer the world has ever seen. But now this dream has passed away, I am even as other women, who love and are beloved, and seek no more.'

'My beloved, this is the sum of life's happiness. Without love life is a mere wilderness. He who goes through life unloved and unloving has wasted his existence.

'The ascetic hopes for great reward when he reaches the Heaven of his desires; but man may make or mar his own Paradise by his own hand. His own course of life shapes it.'

'To me, Swami,' whispered Mercia earnestly, 'it is happiness supreme to know that thou art near. The world may shower its favours, or award its indifference: it is all the same to me. I am satisfied with the knowledge of thy love.'

'And I am mad with joy!' cried Swami passionately, as he covered her face with ardent kisses; the first he had ever bestowed on woman; the first she had ever received from man.

'Once I thought,' she resumed, 'that the tender regard in which I held Geometrus was known by this name. But now mine eyes are opened. I see that Friendship, not Love, inspired my affection. This new emotion hath another birth; a different force behind it: for notwithstanding what has happened this night I feel the same sincere regard for him. His love for me never gave birth to the feeling that thine hath done: for I deliberately disregarded it, deeming my work of greater importance. But for thee, Swami, there is nothing I would not do—even to die; for life without thy love would be a living death.'

'Geometrus!' exclaimed Swami, starting at the name: 'In my own great joy I had forgotten his disappointment. His loss is my great gain. I would I could comfort him by making him acquainted with the honourable future that is in store for him. For he will distinguish himself above all in his profession, and the whole world shall honour him.'

'Dear, dear Geometrus, thou dost indeed deserve it!' cried she enthusiastically, for her heart pained at the thought of what his sorrow would be in losing her. 'But tell me, Swami, of my coming glory. Where is this

Empire that I am destined to govern, and how can such a wonderful event be brought about?'

'It is the Empire of India, my sweet one: it is the home of my fathers—my own beautiful country!' he exclaimed rapturously. 'Thou wilt be chosen by the vote of the nation as their first Empress  To thee is given the honour of establishing the Royal Line for India! Thou and I, Mercia; our children, and children's children shall hold the reins of Government through all generations.

'Then will be re-established the sove reignty of my forefathers, who reigned in India five hundred years ago.  When thy coronation takes place will be fulfilled the prophecy of my father's father who predicted that in one hundred years a woman, young, beautiful, and talented, should reign over his country, dwelling with her people in happiness and peace.'

'How can these things be?' mused Mercia, as she clasped her hands together oppressed with this vision of greatness.

'THE GREAT TEST TOURNAMENT is the first

step towards its attainment.  In a few days it is here; victory will be ours, and India will be free to choose her own Ruler.  Leave the rest to God, for thou hast no part in its arrangement.  The honour will be awarded, unsought by thee.'

'I have still all to learn concerning the Administration of this great country,' said she reflectively.  'It is true I am acquainted with its history from a scholar's point of view, but practically I know nothing.

'To rule a people successfully, we should be in perfect sympathy with them; understanding their mode of thought, customs, and prejudices; actually knowing their inner life.

'It is impossible to rule a people justly, and legislate to meet their wants fully and completely, except we be in touch with them throughout.'

'I will teach thee, Mercia, all this,' said Swami eagerly.  'I will be ever at thy side to tell thee all that thou wouldst know.  See,' said he, pointing to his noble tiers of books, for now they were in his library, 'we two will read and study them together, and from those silent teachers of every age gain the piled-up wisdom of numerous generations, in a short space.'

'What a treasury of ancient lore!' exclaimed Mercia, as rising from her seat, she went from tier to tier examining their contents. 'I shall have a continual feast—a daily enjoyment of wonderful Oriental literature, as soon as I have mastered the necessary knowledge of up-to-date administration, which of course, shall have my first attention.'

'And by marking the mistakes of the present Administration, correct thine own,' added Swami, as he gazed lovingly upon her every movement.

Thus conversing far into the night, on this most absorbing topic; to the one, newly-born, and deeply interesting, by reason of its approaching associations; to the other, for its memories of the past; its unsatisfactory present,—from a patriot's point of view,—and its promise of a glorious future, the hours sped away unconsciously; till at length, Mercia felt a languor stealing over her; which Swami perceiving suddenly exclaimed— 'Dearest, thou art wearied. It is not meet to go forth at this hour. Be my guest to-

night, and to-morrow we two will attend the
trial, for now thou art my especial care.'
Then summoning his attendants he bade
them bring in certain refreshments of jellies,
and light wines ; after partaking of which,
the servants conducted her to a richly furnished sleeping-chamber.  Amidst the pearly-
tinted silken sheets, and richly embroidered
coverlet, all delicately perfumed, Mercia sank
into a sound and refreshing slumber, giving
no thought to the trial on the morrow, or the
difficulties her case would present now that
she had practically accepted the king's
pardon, without her counsel's consent.

# CHAPTER XI.

THE next morning when Mercia awoke and found herself in this luxurious bed-chamber, surrounded by every comfort that modern invention could bestow; for every article of utility represented some rare work of art : and every imaginable want was supplied by the most ingenious arrangements ; it seemed to her that she had gone through a series of delightful scenes in a dream of wonderful vividness.

The recollection of the previous evening, in which so much was seen, and so much experienced, made it difficult to believe that it possessed any greater solidity than the pictures in some stereoscopic arrangement. But the great fact that a new and supreme joy reigned in her bosom—that she loved, and was beloved—proved convincing evidence of its reality.  For the first time in her life she felt the supreme happiness—the unutterable joy of this unique exaltation that comes once, or perhaps twice, in a lifetime to every human being.

When she had descended the magnificently carved staircase that led into the reception rooms, she was met by Swami himself, who conducted her into the breakfast-room where an inviting meal was awaiting her. The most nourishing dishes, where the palate and the digestion were equally considered being placed on the table by native servants, as soon as she had put in an appearance, to which she paid fair justice.

She was in excellent spirits; notwithstanding the thought of the ordeal that lay before her; for nothing could damp, or depress them while under the influence of the present bliss, and future dignities promised her.

Swami, too, looked supremely happy. A quiet, suppressed joy beamed in his deep, dreamy eyes, which shed its light over his expressive countenance. His voice too, had a special softness in its tone, that was peculiarly charming to Mercia's sensitive ear.

It was, in truth, the most delightful meal

for these two beings that had been their lot to partake of; the lives of both having been hitherto solitary, laborious, and even ascetic to some extent.

'Now, isn't this delightful!' laughed Mercia, gaily. 'How nice everything tastes when one has good company! King Solomon knew what he was talking about when he uttered oracularly—" Better a dinner of herbs where love is, than the stalled ox," et cetera; but in our case we score heavily, having the enjoyment of both commodities.'

'The proverb holds good all the same;' replied Swami; 'with thee, my Life, the dinner of herbs would be a banquet, for thy face is a continual feast for me; thy presence would sweeten the coarsest fare.'

'When I enter my kingdom, Swami—but there—I cannot realise my future glory—I feel that this is greatness thrust upon me! I cannot conceive why the people of India should think of me—me—a poor astronomer! I have no regal blood in my veins—no glorious ancestry to boast of.

'It is true my mother accomplished some good for the women of India, devoting a great part of her life in the promotion of their welfare; but that can scarcely bring any weight to the balance in my favour, in such a case as this: the whole matter to my mind is inexplicable,' said she reflectively.

Swami smiled, as he watched the puzzled look upon her face, for of course it was all clear enough to him why the people of India had picked her out as the representative of their country's eminence and glory; after a pause, he thought it no harm to tell her somewhat of the situation.

'There are but two topics talked of just now, not only throughout this Empire but the whole world. They form subject for conversation everywhere. The Court; the spirit café, the theatre, the club, the dinner-table; the street corner, the race-course, wherever men congregate, or women either, the chief food for talk is THE GREAT TEST TOURNAMENT, and the impeachment for high treason, of Mercia, the Astronomer Royal, and her two friends—Geometrus, the Assistant Astronomer, and Sadbag the Politician.

'It is well-known how the case stands, for Sadbag gave it to the whole world immediately before his imprisonment. Everyone believes in thine innocence, and the Emperor's guilt. They say he ought to be indicted for perjury—but from his position that is impossible. There are even now hundreds of letters in thy counsel's keeping expressive of the sympathy of every country. France offers thee a similar position in her Empire as that thou hast resigned here, Russia does the same, even before they know the issue of the trial; but when thine innocence is proved beyond dispute, every country will vie with each other in showing thee honour; the only method open to them of displaying their contempt of Felicitas' unworthy conduct. A two-fold motive will inspire India to top them all in glorifying thee. One is sincere admiration for thy character and attainments, the other is the punishment of their country's tyrant, by the promotion of one he sought to ruin ; for it was Felicitas' influence which made the WORLD's TRIBUNAL TRIAL of no account for India.

'For this reason they do not bless him—they curse him by electing thee—his enemy—an enemy of his own making—for of all men thou shouldst despise him utterly.'

'I do heartily despise him—he's the meanest cur I know,' remarked Mercia excitedly; 'he is capable of saying anything to save his own skin: he had scarcely finished protesting how much he loved me, when to suit the situation he turned round and made a false charge against me, and my two friends who were witnesses of my innocence.'

'That matches my experience of him to a tee,' returned Swami, who was growing quite communicative with Mercia. 'He came yesterday to have his fortune told; he wished to learn the issue of the trial, hoping all would go well with him. I showed him the principal phases of the trial, projected on the psychic-plate beneath the stereoscopic crystal, the sight of which made him boil with anger—he was vexed beyond description, and for my pains in bringing out these splendid psycho-developments I only got his growlings to the effect that he wished he had never troubled himself at all to seek my aid. "Thou wouldst have me curse, when I can only bless," said I, and gave him good counsel, at which he fumed impatiently. But of all vacillating hounds, I think he takes the cake. One moment love, or rather desire, then fear, envy, revenge, swayed him by turns : he changed about like a weathercock moved by every wind.

'However, fear was uppermost in his mind, all through, and reached its climax when he beheld the pictures, so finally he decided to take his flight to Berlin where he intends remaining until the trial be well over, and all its attendant gossip grown stale, *as he hopes.*

'But the 1st of May will bring him back ; he cannot miss the GREAT TEST TOURNAMENT which quickly follows to-day's event. Both will end disastrously for him, and none will say " he's sorry." '

'I'm sorry I can't feel sorry either,' remarked Mercia laughingly. 'But Swami, I must away now, and explain to my counsel this new aspect of affairs. He must be prepared for the changes that have taken place last night—the Emperor's withdrawal of the suit ; his flight, and my discharge from prison. It is necessary that he be made acquainted with these altered conditions, and shape his course accordingly.'

'My carriage is in readiness for thee,

Mercia, at any moment thou art ready to depart.  Shall I accompany thee, or no?'

'I would prefer seeing him alone, dear Swami, I am not prepared to make my lawyer my confessor, as would be almost necessary if I were in thy company at such a time.  But I count upon thy presence near me at the trial, for few are my friends.  I have led the life of a recluse almost, so great has been my devotion to my work, and this is how that ingrate has rewarded me.  Farewell, dearest, for one hour only—in that time I will see thee at the court.'  And Mercia stepping into the well-appointed carriage belonging to Swami was driven away to the barrister's.

# CHAPTER XII

THE Great Justice Hall, as it was named, was of such dimensions that it afforded accommodation for several thousands of persons, who on this occasion of unprecedented interest availed themselves of it without delay. A long line of carriages containing the *élite* of society awaited the opening of the great door with that admirable spirit of patience which the aristocracy display on great occasions. A few of these vehicles were drawn by horses, but most were impelled by electric motive force.

A *queue* of persons who kept no ' carriage steerer,' doing their own driving usually, had come on foot, and had taken their places in the order of their arrival, for the indecent rioting and pushing for priority of places at the doors of public buildings was put down by this time, a lady member of Parliament having brought a bill to make this unruly behaviour punishable as street-brawling.

By the time the Court was opened every available seat was filled, not only by the *élite* of the Empire, but by members of the Continental aristocracy also; including two Crowned Heads among their number. On all great occasions, when a crush was expected, the public were admitted by ticket, which could be obtained by application to the Usher, who issued no greater number than the accommodation afforded.

The Emperor Nicholas, the Fourth, of Russia, accompanied by his Empress; the newly-crowned Emperor, Louis XX., of France, occupied seats set apart for the *crême de la crême* of the aristocracy.

It was, in point of fact, attended by a crowd of great personages, whose importance could not admit of their presence at any ordinary affair, however swift the means of locomotion lessened the inconvenience of travel.

It was not every day that an Emperor appeared in the witness box, and on such an unparalleled occasion it was necessary to make an effort and not miss such a rare treat.

Then Mercia, herself, had occupied such a high position in everybody's estimation that the charge against her of High Treason, by her threatened assault on the sacred person of his Majesty, gave a piquancy to the affair which no vulgar assassin could have afforded. Besides, those ' in the know,' expected to hear evidence so deliciously spicy that to miss it would have been barbarity. Foreign journals having given strong hints of the situation in their gossiping columns, inspired by Sadbag's telegrams to the secretaries of clubs in various cities, including several continental clubs among their number.

Of course the newspapers circulating in the Teutonic Empire were much too circumspect to hint at the true aspect of the affair. To have anticipated evidence; or to have expressed an opinion on a case still pending would have led to serious difficulties, proving most embarrassing to the proprietors. Consequently, a distracting shade of mystery surrounded the coming trial, making it particularly attractive to everybody.

Whilst awaiting the proceedings, the anxious auditory amused themselves by giving expression to their private opinions, which no law of libel at any period of social history has been found powerful enough to repress.

'What glorious fun!' cried the young sprig of nobility, 'Felicitas falling out with his lady Astronomer. I wouldn't miss it for worlds!'

'What a disgraceful episode in the annals of Royalty!' remarked the elderly prude, who was evidently as anxious as the fastest of swell-ocracy to listen to the forthcoming details.

'I wouldn't be Mercia for millions! It is altogether frightful to have such dealings with a MAN!' exclaimed the serious young lady; who showed her abhorrence of such indecency by bringing her opera glasses to scan the scene more critically.

'The Emperor has done quite right, to make a stand against the machinations of rabid Republicans;' remarked a staunch Royalist. 'We won't know where we are if this kind of thing goes unpunished. It is evident on the face of it that it is a conspiracy to lower the Imperial prestige, so as to pave the way for a Republic, when the government of the Empire would become a hotbed of office seekers, rivalling America of a hundred years ago, whose motto was,—" National good go hang, we'll feather our nest while we may." '

'This comes of the preposterous advancement of women : had the Astronomer Royal been a *man* such a scene could not have occurred,' observed an acidulated Science-failure of the male sex, whose ill-success at competitive exams. had rendered vicious.

'If it be a political intrigue, as the Royalist journals aver, how can sex affect her loyalty ? The same might have happened with a variation, had the Astronomer Royal been of the male sex,' returned his neighbour.

'It is a love-intrigue, ending with the usual quarrel,' whispered an elderly Solomon, wise in the knowledge of the world's weakness.

'I thought Mercia incapable of love-intrigues, or any other, being a perfect model of all the virtues,' answered his neighbour.

'All women are " perfect " till they're tried,' uttered the same cynic dryly.

'Which means that Mercia is no better than she should be,' laughed another.

'Perhaps she was *too* good,' remarked a third.

'Which way?' inquired his friend, poking him with his elbow.

'That the evidence must show,' replied another of the coterie.

'Was there ever a case where the honest, downright truth was given on either side? I never knew one,' emphatically declared another of the group. 'It has been the same through all time,' he added after a pause, 'for an eminent judge of the nineteenth century averred that throughout the whole course of his long experience on the woolsack he had never come across a case where the evidence was not, in more or less degree, suppressed.'

'The world's stage keeps pretty much the same all through the piece; humanity is very human yet;' sighed a white-haired old gentleman, with a very sweet expression on his countenance.

'It will be *sinfully* disappointing if the

case is hushed up,' whispered one man to his neighbour, in another part of the Hall. 'The Emperor is *non est* : he has *bunked* ! '

'What! Has he fled? Impossible! He dare not do so. *He* threw the gauntlet, and must abide the issue. He *cannot* run away,' returned his friend who was bewildered with amazement.

' All the same, he is off, gone to Berlin on important State affairs, leaving word that the trial could be abandoned altogether, or take its chance without him.'

'I hope it won't be permitted to fall through,' cried the other man excitedly; ' it would be monstrous after all this fuss, and preparation.'

'I cannot find an adjective in our language strong enough to express *my* disappointment if it collapse. I want to see Mercia righted; she is honour and probity itself, and the opportunity of clearing her character should not be denied her, notwithstanding the absence of her accuser.'

'See,' said his friend, ' the Empress is taking her seat near Nicholas of Russia, that looks healthy—she is doubtless expecting a *dénouement* of which she wishes to be the witness.'

'But there is no Felicitas to escort her, that proves the account of his flight to be trustworthy.'

'I wish her joy of the situation,' remarked an all-knowing one; 'she'll wish a thousand times over she had kept away.'

Just before the great clock pointed at half-past ten, disengaged barristers, who came to see and hear for the sake of gaining experience, took their appointed seats, for this custom was formally recognised.

Counsel engaged in the case, arrayed in gown and wig, appeared also, whose capabilities were freely discussed by the onlookers.

But, when Mercia, escorted by the renowned Swami entered the Hall, so universal was the feeling in her favour, that a great burst of applause greeted her appearance.

It was as spontaneous as it was unusual, for that great mass appeared to be moved by one emotion, which could only find utterance by an intense roar of hand-clapping; signifying as plainly as if delivered in so many words—' Mercia, we believe in thee: before we hear thy defence we feel in our hearts that thine is a just cause, and thou art good and true to the core!'

Mercia raised her eyes, and looking round at the assembled people, smiled sweetly, and bowed her head in acknowledgment of the sympathy accorded her; while attendant ushers vainly called for silence, deeming it their duty to put down all demonstrations of approval.

She was attired in a rich crimson velvet gown that fell in graceful folds from her shapely shoulders; the hue of which lent a deeper rose-tint to her cheeks, whose colour had somewhat paled during her incarceration.

But what appeared most inexplicable to the multitude was the expression of serene sweetness that overspread her countenance. It was indeed an indefinable expression, indicating a variety of emotions. Joy, content, intense happiness, and possession, all united in imparting to her face a look of subdued and silent triumph; but he who could gaze beneath the surface might have read that LOVE, all conquering LOVE had made his home in her bosom, and through her brilliant eyes, illumined with a divine radiance those windows of her soul.

All bent their gaze upon her. The noble stature ; the perfectly moulded form ; the well-shaped head ; the exquisite beauty of every feature, lighted by that divine expression which shone from out her star-like eyes, brought a murmur of admiration, and suppressed enthusiasm from every side.

All through the Hall it spread itself; and Swami perceived that in those millions of brain-waves floating round him, admiration for the woman who held his soul was the one prevailing emotion.

After the first burst of enthusiasm had subsided Swami himself came in for notice.

'Dayanand Swami! The great thought-reader!' exclaimed different persons *sotto voce*, as each one recognised him.

'Whoever saw the Eastern Hermit in a public place before? What means this strange innovation?'

'Now this is getting mysterious,' observed Prince Osbert gaily to his neighbour, Louis, of France, 'our great Magician escorting our fair

Astronomer—what in the name of goodness is going to happen?'

'Beauty holds Magic, all the world over, and star-gazing and thought-reading complete the full magician,' answered the French monarch gallantly.

'I bet she's been to get her fortune told, and Swami, like the rest of us, has succumbed. But no fellow has the shadow of a chance with her; she's gone on Geometrus, that melancholy being sitting yonder. He's the cause of all the row,' whispered Osbert oracularly, 'but for him our cousin Felicitas might not have fared so badly. However, 'tis better so ; 'tis time his wings were clipped.'

'All the world avers,' returned Louis earnestly, 'that this beauteous being is a slave to Duty. Day and night, year in, year out, she's ever at her post, and gives no thought to love, the essence of existence.'

While these observations were going on, the three Judges, attired as in days of old, took their seats with suitable solemnity, when the Court opened with the same formularies as had been in use for hundreds of years: for the Courts of Law more than any other institution cling to the ancient order of things with tenacity.

Even the old-fashioned blunder of saying ' you ' for ' thee ' was still adhered to in the Law Courts, verbal innovations being equally discountenanced.

After a short delay the auditory was startled by hearing the charge delivered, of which the following is the substance.

' Mercia Montgomery, you are charged with feloniously attempting the life of His Imperial Majesty, Albert Felicitas, Supreme Ruler and Governor of Great Britain and Ireland, Emperor of the Teutonic, Indian, and African Empires, which murderous attempt is accounted HIGH TREASON by the law of these Realms.   Do you plead Guilty or not Guilty ? '

Before the accused could possibly have time to give her answer, the Public Prosecutor interfered.

' I am empowered to convey to the prisoner the favour of his Imperial Majesty's clemency. Taking into consideration the prisoner's long and valuable service rendered to her country, also the great loyalty she has ever evinced towards her Sovereign during that period of faithful service, the Emperor has decided to overlook the sudden outburst of passion made by his otherwise faithful subject, and illustrious Astronomer, and has therefore conveyed to her his Royal Pardon, in proper form, forthwith.

'The prisoner has been already made acquainted with this fact and was in the enjoyment of her freedom last evening,' he added, regarding Mercia with a glance full of meaning.

Then Mercia, motioning her counsel to keep his seat a moment longer, and rising to her full height, replied in low but emphatic tones—'Being altogether innocent of the crime of which I am charged, I am unable to accept the clemency offered by his Most Gracious Majesty.

'It will be soon enough to pray for pardon when I am proved guilty. If the Court will permit, I beg that the trial proceed, and my character for ever cleared from all unworthy imputations.

'I, Mercia, the Astronomer, must leave this Court with my name pure, unsullied, and

honourable; or hide my head in shame for
ever.'

'Long live Mercia! Long live Mercia!'
resounded in mighty force throughout that
great Hall. The whole multitude was with
her in one intense wave of sympathy; for she
had given utterance to their own feeling.
They desired to bottom the whole business,
and place their beloved Astronomer on the
proud pedestal she had formerly occupied.

Besides, the Englishman's love of justice
was another factor in the case, and no matter
what the issue, they desired to see fair play
throughout.

Swami looked radiant with happiness as
he pressed towards her side eager to render
her whatever trifling service possible at such
a moment.

Geometrus wore a serious and downcast
aspect, as if he believed that nothing would
go right. Sadbag sitting near him, with a
mysterious parcel by his side, seemed the
picture of suppressed satisfaction.

When everybody had quieted down
Mercia's counsel got upon his legs, and requested that the Public Prosecutor should

state his case, to which demand the Judges agreed. Thereupon, the Emperor's counsel made his charge according to the manner in which he had been instructed, but having no witnesses to produce, save Prince Osbert, who averred he saw nothing, from which testimony no amount of questioning could make him depart, the Defence was commenced without delay.

Rising to his feet Mercia's counsel proceeded with his speech.

'To-day I am placed in a position as painful to me as a subject, as it is unique in the annals of a Law Court. Painful, insomuch as it is necessary for the ends of justice that I shall have to accuse my Sovereign of conduct so base that the meanest subject of his Realms would blush to be found guilty of the like.

'I am in a position to show that the Emperor's visits to his Astronomer were not made either in the interests of science, or those of his subjects: no such justifiable, or worthy motives prompted his course of action. On the contrary, these interviews were made with the intention of corrupting her pure mind, and of guiling her away from her duty.

' By his artful insinuations he endeavoured
to gradually lead her on to disregard her vows
of abstention from Love, or Marriage, with a
view of paving the way for his own purposes.
He dwelt upon the folly of continuing a course
of asceticism, whose only effect would be
ultimately, a serious injury to her health and
happiness ; and she in the perfect innocence
of her pure mind, accepted it at the moment,
as a piece of fatherly advice that should not
be disregarded.

' Like the Eastern fable of Eve and the
Serpent, she listened to the voice of the
Tempter not knowing he was planning her
downfall.  But luckier than our First Mother,
Mercia discovered her mistake before touching
the forbidden fruit.

' From the evidence you will learn that the
Tempter used every argument he could think
of, offering the possible and the impossible
to induce her to comply.  At length, with a
heart bursting with mortification and indignation she essayed to leave him, when he
endeavoured to forcibly detain her ; upon
which she raised her ebony life-preserver to
warn him from trespassing on her person.

At this juncture he was surprised by the entrance of the Prince and Geometrus, who were amazed at a scene so unexpected. Mortified at being caught at such a moment he tried to explain away the difficulty, and coolly turned the tables upon the lady, by accusing her of some failure in duty; at this moment who should emerge from a corner of the apartment, which was partially concealed by a large screen, but Mr. Sadbag, whose presence it will be my duty to explain.

'It appears that this gentleman having just purchased a phonograph, constructed on a new principle, and being wishful to present it to one of his grand-children, as a scientific plaything, he carried it to Mistress Mercia with a view of obtaining a record of her conversation, which he expected would prove equally instructive, as interesting to his grand-children.

'It was his intention to ask this favour, as soon as she made her appearance, and in order that her time, usually so valuable, should not be unduly taken up, he opened out his instrument, making it ready for the reception of the sound-waves. Finding, at length, that he would have to wait some little time before seeing her, he took up a book and commenced reading, and finished by dozing off into a light slumber, according to the manner of elderly folk with nothing to occupy their attention.

'He was awakened from his sleep by the sound of voices,—that of the Emperor, and the fair Astronomer; both evidently in a state of unusual excitement.

'To his utter annoyance he discovered that the nature of the conversation to which he was being made an unwilling listener, was of a character wholly unsuitable for the presence of a third person. The situation became more and more distressing to him; he knew not what to do. It was impossible to leave the apartment without discovery; it was equally objectionable to reveal his presence at such a moment. With many conflicting thoughts, he finally decided to stay where he was until the termination of the interview, when he would leave the room comfortably; at the same time forming a resolution to keep the affair a dead secret within his own bosom, and let it rest there for ever.

'This merciful intention on his part towards the Emperor, he was compelled to abandon, on account of the false charge that monarch had so quickly and ingeniously invented against Mercia, whereby he hoped to cover his guilt.

'I will now call upon Mr. Sadbag to open his instrument, and give us the dialogue that was so unintentionally recorded therein; but which I am afraid will prove more interesting to the company present, than edifying or instructive to that gentleman's progeny.'

Mr. Sadbag immediately sprang to his feet, and taking up the mysterious parcel proceeded to the witness box, when he requested a few moments' grace to adjust the mechanism of his unique witness; after which was heard in the most natural tones the voice of the Emperor in lively mood saying—'Ah, Mistress Mercia, what cheerful looks thou dost carry to-day! Methinks thy face betokens much content: hast thou taken my words to heart, fair lady, 'twas truly excellent advice?'

Then followed Mercia's musical voice, in this wise—'Sire, thou saidst something concerning the sun. Thou didst talk of coming to learn more of his condition, I believe.'

Then followed a little laugh, half satirical, half good-humoured from Felicitas, after which the machine said—' I fain would know more of the sun's late vagaries: but it would please me infinitely better to learn something of thyself. Dost thou never feel lonely?'

Here a suppressed titter went round the Court, but the machine heeded it not.

'Often enough, Sire,' it said in Mercia's sweet tones, 'the hours speed away at times very quickly when I am hard at work; but when it is time to rest then the feeling of solitude overwhelms me. I get appalled at the silence that surrounds me, and a melancholy seizes me so severely, that I rise unable to cope with my duties.'

'Art thou then tired of this occupation? It is indeed too much for thee. Rest a while, sweet Mercia, and let the stars take care of themselves for a season.'

The voice of the machine grew quite pathetic here: evidently Felicitas was growing sympathetic.

'Oh, that would spoil all my calculations,' said the machine, very sweetly, 'the work of years would be as nought were I to stay my hand now. No, I will wait until my treatise on the stars is complete; then I will take some little change for my health's sake.'

'Health and love, sweet Mercia, go hand in hand together,' the machine sang out in melting tones, 'let thine heart soften to its influence, and all will go well with thee. Thy melancholies will disappear; thy solitude lightened, for thou wilt have a new theory to analyse—a new and a better one. Yes, thou canst love, Mercia, I know it; for thine eyes were made for the conquest of man's heart, rather than star-gazing. Cease to disregard the designs of Nature when she formed thee, and give thyself unto the pleasure of love.'

'Sire,' answered Mercia's sweet voice, which now had a strange, startled tone—'I know not what answer to give in this matter —I am yet unprepared—perplexed with this reasoning of thine.'

'Hast thou not felt the want of companionship, dear Mercia? Here penned in this solitude only fit for a greybeard thou dost pine, yet knoweth not what it is ails thee. It is good to be loved, fair one, to realise how much thy womanhood means. Hast thou never felt its joys—its pains?' asked the voice in a coaxing sort of tone.

'But my bond, Sire, I cannot break my bond, signed by my own hand, to forswear love and marriage: no one but thyself can relieve me of this obligation,' replied Mercia's voice excitedly.

'I heartily relieve thee, then, my good Mercia: I care not for the bond one iota, if that be all that's in thy way. Keep thy post, as thou likest thy work so well, and enjoy the delights of love at the same time,' reeled out the machine in the Emperor's most insinuating tones.

Then followed a low cry of joy, in Mercia's voice, and the sound of a kiss; listening ladies blushed, smart young men sniggered, and elderly men looked as if things were getting serious.

'Isn't that machine playing it low on the lady?' whispered Prince Osbert to Louis, his neighbour.

'Hush,' returned the French Emperor—

' listen, there's a volley of kisses going off—be quiet, pray ! '

' It's getting beyond a joke—it really is ! Just look at the Empress, she's gone green in the face !  Mercia's looking pretty pink, and altogether the matter is too blue for my modesty ! ' exclaimed the Prince, while bursting with suppressed mirth.

All eyes regarded the beautiful culprit seated in the witness box with increased interest.  ' Oh, thou guilty creature—think shame to thyself ! ' the ladies' looks said as plainly as possible.

' He's having a good time of it ! ' whispered one to his neighbour.

' She's no better than she should be, after all ! ' muttered another.

' Such pretty lips were made for kissing ! ' remarked another jocularly.

' So it seems ! ' answered his neighbour dryly.

' Felicitas hasn't bad taste ! ' cried another.

' He knows how to do it ! ' was the rejoinder.

' Most entertaining, truly,' remarked a lady sarcastically.

'Entertaining isn't the word for it—'tis scrumptious!' returned her husband. 'One hears the kisses, and sees the lady; 'tis a treat for the gods!'

'Oh, the hussy! Don't look at her. What a cheek, to face it out like this!'

These various remarks, and many more besides, occupied but a few seconds for delivery, for the Usher calling out silence, on hearing the low murmur of voices, the machine began talking again.

'What means the Emperor by this un-heard-of liberty? What have I done that I should be treated as a courtesan by my Sovereign?' cried the machine, in a voice choked with pain and indignation.

'A courtesan!' repeated the Emperor's voice, 'I would give thee a crown if I could! Thy queenly brow was truly made for one. And by the stars, thou shalt have it yet! Yes, dear Mercia, thou shalt share my throne, and rule me, my sweet, together with mine Empire.'

'Share thy throne and rule thine Empire! Surely, Sire, thou hast gone mad!'

'Yes, truly, I am mad—mad with love

for thee, and thou knowest it, Mercia, else wouldst thou have kissed my hand in acknowledgment of it?'

'In acknowledgment of *thy* love!' cried the machine scornfully. 'It was not so—*thy* love never entered my thought.'

'Whose then?'

'Geometrus,' said the instrument, in Mercia's soft voice.

'Geometrus!' scoffed the machine in the Emperor's tones. 'And dost thou place that poltroon before *me*? Am I to be flouted for *him*?'

'His love is honourable, and thine is not; therein lies the difference, my Sire,' the voice of Mercia replied in a propitiating tone; as if to win the monarch over to give consent to her marriage with Geometrus.

'But my love *shall be made honourable*, Mercia, I will get a divorce, and thou shalt fill the Empress' place. Aye, and fill it far away better than she has ever done! I hate her—curse her!' Then followed a grating noise as if the Emperor were grinding his teeth in fury at the thought of his marriage fetters. A painful feeling spread itself through the Court; the Empress became the cynosure of all eyes: her face turned deathly white; a minute later she had fainted, and was carried away from the scene that jealousy had prompted her to witness.

'But I cannot rob another woman of her husband: I would not defraud the meanest in thy realms, still less thine Empire's highest lady!' uttered the machine in pure clear tones.

A suppressed murmur of applause greeted this avowal, but the machine went on heedless of interruption.

'It is not robbery, Mercia, she doth not own my heart, and never did! I was cozened into the marriage by my cousin Osbert—curse him, for a meddling fool!'

'He did it, doubtless, for the best. The whole of thy Cabinet approved, so did the nation. It is a new thing for me to learn that our Emperor lives unhappily with his spouse —I cannot understand it.'

'She's trying to reason him out of his folly,' remarked Louis, of France, 'good little girl!'

'I never felt the chains gall till now, Mercia,' the machine confessed with relentless veracity. 'A quiet indifference kept me content until thy beauty set my heart a-beating with a new joy. I knew not love till mine eyes dwelt upon thy loveliness, and mine ears listened to the words that flowed from thy lips like a sweet rippling fountain; whose waters gave forth a pure, clear, life-giving stream.

'Yes, I have drunk therein, and am filled with new emotions—new joys—new hopes— new life!' The phonograph here made a pause, when it recommenced with a sobbing sound.

'Now is my beauty an evil thing, and a curse to me!' cried Mercia's voice, in soft, pathetic sweetness. 'Would I had never been born, or that Nature had shaped me uncomely, for then this misfortune could not have overtaken me! Two men desire me, and I may not have either. I must live in a world filled like a garden with flowers— flowers and blossoms of love. Yet, I may not touch them; their fragrance is not for me; not one may I wear on my breast!

'Yet, they nod and beckon me to pluck them. They offer me the incense of their being, and would fain spend their full fragrance upon me; for their desire is to nestle on my bosom, and give me the joy of their beauty and love.'

As the instrument gave utterance to this sweet rhapsody, delivered in a low, clear, plaintive voice, that fell like music on the ear of the enraptured auditory, who listened breathlessly to every word that fell from her lips, as it were; for in imagination they saw her with bowed head, and clasped hands breathing the poetry of that moment of divine exaltation.

The human desire for human love was finding expression: the longing of the soul for companionship was shaping itself into language so intensely irresistible, that it went to every heart with the fleetness of the lightning's flash.

Only one feeling prevailed throughout that great assembly—admiration for the noble character of the beautiful woman sitting there before them, whose flushed cheek and lowered eyelids, evidenced the modesty of her womanhood.

As soon as a pause was reached by the instrument, the enthusiasm of the people could be restrained no longer. Men testified their approval in true English fashion by the heartiest round of applause as was never before heard in that soberly-conducted Justice Hall. When the excitement had somewhat subsided, Mercia rose to her feet, and turning her gaze with an air of modest dignity upon the people, she addressed them.—

'Dear friends—until this moment, I knew not I possessed so many——'

Another round of applause.

'Dear friends,' she continued sweetly, ' accept my warmest thanks for your generosity in believing in me while yet I remained unheard. My lords,' and she turned to the presiding Judges, ' it is true that this instrument,' she pointed then to the phonograph— ' has been signally instrumental in rendering undeniable testimony of the value of the evidence placed before you. Nevertheless, I knew not when I came hither that I was to encounter my own words uttered without thought, or preparation, in a moment of excitement ; for probably, had I been aware that such was my friend, Mr. Sadbag's intention, my place at this justice bar would never have been filled.

· Holding his Majesty's " pardon " as I do, I was under no necessity to appear before you, and plead the justice of my cause. Nevertheless, I do not regret the exposure, for after all, it has given the opportunity, to you, dear people, of showing the good feeling you entertain for me.

' I felt in my heart when I elected to go forward with my defence that the people of this great Empire would render me justice and see me safely through this trying ordeal.'

' Good people,' exclaimed Mr. Sadbag, smiling good-humouredly, ' pray don't applaud any more ; I can't get along with my talking-machine ; and until I finish the Court is unable to arrive at a decision. 'Tis a pity to hinder the Emperor's pretty speeches, just listen to this, and see how poetical he is : the tender passion makes even kings grow quite tragical.'

' Mercia, Mercia, give me thy love !  Take me, my beloved, spurn me no longer, for without thee I am as one dead.  As a world without sun, without life, without warmth I shall go on my way darkened for ever.

' Take me into the sunshine of thy love ;

give me new life, dearest; resuscitate and refresh me with the joy of thy beauty, and let us drink of the wine of Love's pleasures for ever.

'Then shall we two learn how good it is to love; how sweet it is to be together! How delightful the blending of two souls made satisfied with their own companionship!'

'It is Geometrus who speaks,' came the soft dreamy tones of Mercia, 'Geometrus has opened his heart to me at last!'

'Geometrus!' shouted the machine in the angry tones of the Emperor, 'it is *not* Geometrus; it is I—Felicitas—Felicitas thine Emperor, who abjectly offers thee his love; his crown, and sues thee, Mercia, his servant —his astronomer.'

Then Mercia awakening, evidently, from her love-dream, and realising her true position exclaimed with great dignity, 'Felicitas, the Emperor, hath no crown to offer his subject, Mercia, for it sits already on the brow of his Royal Spouse. Neither has he love to offer his astronomer, for it is sworn to his Empress for ever. It is an insult to me, Mercia, thine offer of illicit love and I refuse to longer remain in thy service.'

'That will do, Mr. Sadbag,' interrupted the senior Judge, 'we have heard quite sufficient to enable us to arrive at a decision. The prisoner—I mean the accused, is found NOT GUILTY of the charge against her. The lady and her friends may now leave the Court without a stain on their character. It is unnecessary to go into the charges brought against these gentlemen, as the clearing of the principal defender establishes the innocence of the whole three. This case ought never to have come before the Court at all.'

'Good!' exclaimed Sadbag to his trusty phonograph, 'thy testimony is worth more than a score of witnesses, or a Court full of lawyers; thou hast served us well, little one; thanks to Edison, or whoever it was invented thee!'

'Three cheers, three times over for Mercia, the Astronomer Royal!' shouted a stentorian voice, and the tremendous volume of sound was caught up by the thousands who were awaiting the verdict in the streets, and all the city shouted—'Hurrah! Hurrah! Hurrah!' nine times in succession, and women wept for joy, and wreaths were showered upon her, and all the homage due to a great hero was rendered her, just as Felicitas had seen pictured in the psycho-development the day before.

Swami had prepared the carriage and horses for her use, which now stood in readiness. But the climax of the ovation was reached when the people, not knowing what to do to show her honour, removed the prancing steeds, which were startled by the clamour, and drew the chariot themselves.

Publicly, in presence of the crowd, and of her intimate friends, Swami stepped up to the carriage, already piled with laurel wreaths intermixed with flowers of rare beauty, and presented her with his wonderful crown of precious jewels. It represented a wreath of glittering blossoms intertwined with bay leaves; which sparkled with a thousand rays in the bright sunshine; placing this brilliant trophy of that day's triumph on her head he took his seat beside her.

A deeper flush of pleasure came into

Mercia's radiant face, for her happiness was now complete in having him near.

'Three cheers for Swami our great thought-reader and Mercia's friend!' cried one of the crowd, who had seen Swami escort her into the Court, and thereby deduced that he was her most trusty friend.

The people willingly accorded him the acclamation, giving a share also to Geometrus, and the intrepid Sadbag.

But before all this took place, when she was about to leave the Court, crowds of those present gathered round, and gave her their sincere congratulations.

Among these were the Emperor Nicholas of Russia, and the newly-crowned Emperor of France, for that country having grown tired of a republic, imitated America in this respect.

Even Prince Osbert, the cousin of Felicitas, offered Mercia his congratulations; but not an atom of sympathy was expressed for the absent Emperor, though many sincerely pitied his wife.

The Empress of Russia, not satisfied with mere hand-shaking, kissed Mercia warmly, as she exclaimed—'Noble Mercia, then thou wouldst not accept the offer of Felicitas, and discrown my dear daughter—thou wearest already the brightest crown, that of pure virtue. May God ever bless, and reward thee.'

'I'll make Felicitas pay for this!' muttered the Emperor Nicholas to himself, 'his conduct both as an Emperor and husband is disgraceful.'

'There is no occasion for thy Majesty to trouble further in the matter,' observed Swami, 'thy son-in-law hath received his lesson, and will prove, in time, a model husband. Parental responsibilities will make him the most virtuous of monarchs living.'

'Then my daughter will have children?' inquired the Empress eagerly.

'Even so,' answered Swami, smiling, as he turned to lead Mercia away to her carriage.

All along the drive to Greenwich the people took up the glad shout of triumph; but upon Mercia's arrival there, who was accompanied by Swami and Geometrus only, for Sadbag had been carried off by his own political and personal friends, she found that

handsome triumphal arches had been erected
to do her honour, in loyal anticipation of her
victory.

Mercia's eyes filled at this warm tribute
of the people's affection ; while Swami pressed
her hand and whispered that this was as nothing
compared with what awaited her in the very
near future. Geometrus, in the meantime,
overhearing what was said, looked perfectly
petrified with astonishment, as each feature
of the situation was developed.

As the events of the day unfolded themselves his mind became almost a whirligig of
wonder and excitement. He could not understand the presence of Swami at all, at the
trial ; for he knew that up to then Mercia
was entirely unacquainted with him. But
what appeared to him as misplaced as it was
unwelcome, was the part Swami was taking
in the ovation, by whose personality he felt
himself completely overshadowed.

' Who is this Anglo-Indian that I should
have to play second fiddle to him ? ' thought
Geometrus to himself, ' why does Mercia
occupy herself with *him* ? '

From the talking-machine he had learnt

to his infinite joy, of Mercia's love for him ;
it was the first intimation he had received
of her affection, but before he could drink in
the delight of his unexpected bliss, it was
melting away like a dream.

All her attention was engrossed by this
Swami. When she was not engaged giving
her graceful acknowledgments to the enthusiastic crowd, her eyes were looking into his
with that soul-worship, which women accord,
when they have met their ideal.

'She never gazed into my face with that
fervour,' he thought, ' she loves him, else how
could she be so devoted? I have loved her
for years, and this is the reward of my
constancy ; in one day a stranger has ousted
me. This comes of over-cautiousness ; had
I been reckless of consequences, Mercia would
have been mine by this time, made safe by
bonds of wedlock. But I hesitated, believing
her position had greater charms for her than
matrimony. And now—well, no one can
bottom a woman's heart, or gather its meaning. I imagined I was consulting her best
interests when I refrained from declaring my
love, leaving over the matter for time to

put things right.   And this is the result ; a stranger has accomplished more in one day than I with all my years of opportunity.   It is inexplicable.

' However, I'll wait no longer, this night shall conclude the matter.   Ere another day elapses I will have asked her to share my poor fortunes ;   surely we two can meet with appointments as teachers of astronomy and make a respectable livelihood between us. It isn't a very brilliant position to offer, but she will then be mine legally, and no man can take her from me.   My prudence has made me play the fool, so far, but this night shall I learn my fate.   I will delay no longer. Mercia has told the whole world of her preference for me, how then can she have the face to refuse me ? '

As these thoughts passed through Geometrus' mind whilst seated near Swami, the latter looked into his face and remarked impressively—

' The chances and changes of this mortal life are never ending.   They bring sorrow to one, and joy to another.   Strange arrangement this of Fortune ; one moment bestowing good, the next evil. If thou shouldst regard thyself illused to-day, learn that a morrow will come when thou shalt be made content; but not in the manner that is in thine heart at this moment.'

'There is *nothing* that can bring me content, Swami,' replied Geometrus bitterly, 'but that which thou seekest to deprive me of.'

Mercia at this moment was oblivious of the nature of their conversation, her attention having been engaged by the arrival of friends to congratulate her.

When the party reached the Observatory Swami expressed his intention of returning; and as soon as he had assisted Mercia to alight, he conducted her to her sitting-room.

'Take a rest, my beloved,' he whispered softly, 'it will refresh thee; to-morrow I will come and stay awhile beside thee; when I trust thy friend Geometrus will not favour us with his presence. Evidently, by his dark looks he would fain annihilate me, if that were possible.'

'Ah, yes,' returned Mercia, with a sigh and a smile intermixed; 'we two must have explanations. That talking-machine has made things awkward for me. But for that tell-tale instrument I owed him no apologies, seeing that the nature of our friendship had never been discussed between us. Since then I have learnt that which the concentrated wisdom of all the schools could not impart by theory; for it is the realisation and knowledge of what the poets of all ages have made their universal theme; but experience only can reveal the reality.'

'And it is as fresh to us as if utterly unknown hitherto! It is our new discovery!' cried Swami in a rapture as he caught her in his arms.

'But we can't take out a patent for it!' Mercia was in the act of replying, when her words were smothered by the warm kisses pressed upon her lips.

'And must we really part?' exclaimed she, while playfully holding his hands prisoners.

'It will seem an eternity till the morrow,' he murmured, making no effort to escape.

'When I sleep I shall dream of thee, Swami,' and her liquid eyes looked softly into his.

'My day dream shuts out the visions of

the night; for my happiness is too great for the waters of Lethe to cover. With thee to concentre my thought upon, I ask no other refreshment,' uttered Swami softly.

When fame is won, leisure is lost, Mercia quickly discovered; for no sooner had Swami left than she found herself surrounded by crowds of persons who had come to offer their congratulations. Of course the sincerity of those demonstrative ones was not to be doubted, nevertheless the visits of a goodly percentage were prompted more by curiosity to see the woman who might have displaced their Empress, had she been so minded, and the Divorce Courts sufficiently obliging, than anything else. Consequently, Mercia had a livelier time of it for several hours than she was prepared for. People to whom she was a perfect stranger poured in upon her, until at length fairly wearied out with the strain she gave orders to admit no more.

As soon as the apartments were fairly cleared of their visitors she sank down on a sofa exhausted; and was in the act of uttering an exclamation of thankfulness when Geometrus put in an appearance.

'May I have a word with thee?' he asked hesitatingly.

'To-morrow, Geometrus, won't it keep till then?' she said sweetly.

'No, Mercia, I must know my fate to-night, I cannot wait another day. My mind is in such a state of perplexity, that to dream of getting sleep is a folly: I come therefore to sue thee for a good night's rest, and to be made happy for all time;' saying which he took a seat in front of her.

'And how can I make thee comfortable, Geometrus?' laughed Mercia gaily. 'Better take a nerve-soothing tabloid instead of supper, I'll warrant that will give thy mind more rest than anything that I can tell thee.'

'Perhaps it might,' answered he gloomily.

'All the same, I would prefer a hearing if thou wilt grant the favour.'

'Certainly,' she answered with an assumed airiness of manner, for she guessed she was about to go through a bad quarter of an hour, 'now be reasonable, and I will give this matter my best attention,' she added.

'I know I am trespassing upon thy time at an awkward moment,' he went on to say with a certain bitterness in his voice, 'but for all that we will have it out now. What is the meaning of this fortune-telling fellow hanging round thee? What does he want dangling after thee?'

'That is my business,' answered Mercia, suddenly freezing in her manner and turning quite haughty, 'I was not aware that I was answerable to thee in the choice of my friends.'

At this reproof he reddened, and stammered out—

'I did not mean to put it that way,—but I want to know what is this Swami to thee that he should interest himself so greatly in thy affairs?'

'He is my intended husband, Geometrus,' replied Mercia in a low but firm voice. 'I mean to give up my post and marry. He is the only man for whom I could make this sacrifice, as I love my profession greatly. But I love Swami better, and intend to share my fortunes with him whatever they be.'

'And what is to become of me?' inquired Geometrus while his face turned deathly white; 'I thought the phonograph said thou

didst love me.　What am I to think ?　Was
it Swami that filled thy thought when Felicitas
asked the same question ? '

'Of course not,' rejoined Mercia candidly,
· I was unacquainted with him when the
Emperor sought me.　But I will endeavour
to explain it ; otherwise thou mightest arrive
at false conclusions.

'I formed a sincere regard for thee, Geometrus, in the course of these five years that
we have worked together ; and this regard,
owing partly to thy devotion to me, and
partly from a sense of loneliness, the result of
my necessarily solitary mode of life, grew into
such a tender affection that I imagined it was
what people call love.　Consequently, the
notion came into my head that at some time
or other—some day in the distant future, I
would marry thee if such continued to be
thy desire.　But now all those ideas have
been dissipated ; my heart has gone through
a complete revolution, for I have met with
the man for whom I would willingly give up
everything.

'I love him better than all the stars in the
wide universe !　Much as I delighted to gaze

into the Heavens and study with intense interest the wonders of the Celestial depths, yet he is above them all! He is more to me than thousands of worlds! He is nearer and dearer than millions of suns!' cried Mercia with clasped hands, and eyes alight with warm enthusiasm.

'He is certainly *nearer* if propinquity counts for anything;' rejoined Geometrus dryly; 'of course, then, I am to understand that the man who has bowled out the whole Universe, has played it low on me: in other words, I am nowhere *now?*'

'That is so,' said Mercia, 'I now know what love is, for he has taught me, where thou didst fail. Thou hadst no power to impart this knowledge to my understanding. When I look back, I see that Friendship only inspired my thought for thee. I should have continued all my life searching the Heavens. and worrying out the secrets of Nature had I not met my Marrow, my Ideal, my Fate!'

'All three represented in the person of Swami?' added Geometrus cynically.

'Even so,' answered Mercia, taking no notice of his derisive tone. 'In a few days I leave this place, and thou Geometrus canst worthily fill it, and make thy name illustrious for ever.'

'And this is to be the end of my dream!' he burst out in a voice choking with feeling.

'The end of one, and the beginning of another,' returned Mercia, 'thou wilt yet be a great man, whom all men will honour. I leave thee a fair field and a free hand to accomplish this noble ambition.'

# CHAPTER XIII

'The providence that's in a watchful state
Knows almost every grain of Pluto's gold;
Finds bottom in the uncomprehensive deeps;
Keeps pace with thought, and almost like the Gods,
Does thoughts unveil in their dumb cradles.'
*Troilus and Cressida.*

As soon as the trial was concluded,—if the series of extraordinary scenes that took place in the court, could be so designated—the reporters rushed out *en masse* to send their respective phonographs to the editors of the various journals they represented.

Never before had they such a titbit to offer their employers as was now their good luck to possess. A love scene between their Emperor and his astronomer, delivered in a dialogue wherein the actual voices were reproduced was a treat not to be met with every day.

At least a hundred delicate voice-recorders had caught the sound-waves from Sadbag's phonograph, and borrowing the tones of Felicitas and Mercia in their never-to-be-forgotten colloquy, gave them a value unprecedented in all time. As soon as it got abroad that their proprietors were in possession of these treasures, hundreds of speculators offered enormous prices for their purchase, with a view of reeling out their contents to admiring and appreciative audiences throughout the globe.

These offers proved, indeed, too tempting to be resisted, so that in the course of a week or two, India, together with many distant parts, was in the enjoyment of the actual love scene that took place at Greenwich Observatory, the most unlikely of all places for such an incident to happen in.

The Great Test Tournament had been fought and won by the Easterners. Their freedom now achieved, there remained only the nomination and coronation of a Supreme Ruler to go through, the responsibility of which weighed heavily upon the mind of the Indian Parliamentarians.

It was ultimately decided however, that their first Monarch should be elected by the vote of the whole nation, independently of all claims of royal descent made by members of the native aristocracy.

The interesting news of Felicitas' unsuccessful love suit having been brought to the ears of the people so graphically through the medium of the voice-recorders, created an intense excitement in their mind, at all times so sensitive to every emotion.

It brought out Mercia's character in such vivid colours that she appeared to them mentally projected on a living reflector. In their intense imagination, they saw her before them uttering in her melodious dream-like voice her now famous rhapsody ; the tenderness of which appealing to their hearts, stirred up their deepest emotions.

But when they arrived at her indignant refusal of the Emperor's offer to put away his wife, and give her the crown of his Consort, the climax was reached, and the enthusiasm of the people found vent in loud cries of—'MERCIA FOR EVER! LONG LIVE MERCIA, OUR EMPRESS!'

And so the cry spreading itself through every quarter of that vast Empire was caught up in wild delight—LONG LIVE MERCIA, OUR EMPRESS, being echoed from every part, by people of every caste and every creed. But when the intelligence reached this impressionable people that Mercia, the greatest Astronomer, and noblest woman the world had ever seen, was about to enter into a matrimonial alliance with Dayanand Swami, the actual lineal descendant of The Great Mogul Dynasty, which governed India from the early centuries downwards, that settled the question.

In the course of the discussion upon the subject, which took place in the House of Parliament at Calcutta, Sir John Punjaub their well-beloved minister said—'Now is this matter settled to our utmost satisfaction and content. In Dayanand Swami we have the direct descendant of India's greatest, wisest, and most beneficent Ruler, the renowned Abkar, who was the son of Humayun, who was the son of Baber, the founder of the Great Royal Dynasty in the fifteenth century.

'In Dayanand we shall have a second Abkar, for the mantle of his great Ancestor hath fallen on him. In him the people of this great Empire will have a kind Father, a wise Teacher, a just Ruler, and a lover and promoter of learning.

'By the union of Mercia and Dayanand we shall have restored to us the lost Royal Line: in beauteous Mercia, perfect in face, and form, in soul and mind, we have found the true representative of what a monarch ought to be.

'Herein is crystallised the talent, wisdom, and virtue of all generations. In her person we shall have the embodiment of our country's dignity and honour. She shall become the Great Mother of India. The Founder of our Royal Line, and her name shall shine as the stars for ever and ever.'

In the presence of the greatest and most brilliant assemblage India had ever seen since the days of her ancient splendour; consisting of Princes and Potentates richly attired in court dress and coronet, representative of their respective positions of Peishwar, Raja and Maharajah the coronation took place a month later.

By dint of working day and night the pre-

parations for the grand Imperial Procession
to be followed by the Crowning Function,
were completed in that period.

One thousand elephants, richly caparisoned
in cloth of gold and various embroideries;
their heads ornamented with fine filagree
work in gold or silver, interspersed with
gems, according to the wealth of their respective owners, carried the howdahs containing the wives and daughters of the
dignitaries of the Realm.   For Mercia had
issued a mandate beforehand that the ladies
of the Chiefs of the Empire would be expected to take part in the Function, veiled,
or unveiled, according to their respective
ideas of propriety.   In obedience to which
every Ameer, Maharajah, Rajah, Nawab,
Sirdar, Dewan, and Nazim had the ladies of
his family carried in howdahs, where they
enjoyed a splendid view of the situation,
owing to their elevated position, and at the
same time added an Eastern air of gorgeous-
ness to the procession, most impressive to the
eye of the beholder.

The Princes, and native dignitaries themselves followed in carriages drawn by horses,

in the order of their rank the splendidly-appointed Imperial Chariot, containing 'Mercia, The Peerless,' as she was now named, and by her side was seated her Imperial Consort, 'Dayanand, The Wise.'

Long lines of body-guards composed of the finest physiqued men in the realms, attired in a rich uniform of pale blue and gold bearing silver lances, and mounted on high-mettled steeds, preceded and followed the royal chariot, the sight of which drew forth the wildest acclamations of joy from the people.

The ceremony took place neither in Christian nor Hindu temple, but in the great hall of their Parliament House, the most stately building in Calcutta.

As soon as the Coronation Oath was taken by Mercia, in accordance with the custom of their most remote ancestry, she was sprinkled with water from the Ganges, which was contained in a golden bowl glittering with precious jewels. After which, the grand Imperial Crown was placed upon her head by the venerable Prime Minister, who officiated as high priest of the ceremony.

'Now,' said the old man, 'I will finish by quoting a counsel from a part of the most ancient of India's literature,—the Dasakumaracharita, or 'Stories of Ten Princes.'

'Government is an arduous matter; it has three principles; Council, Authority, and Activity. These mutually assisting each other dispatch all affairs. Council determines objects, Authority commences, and Activity effects their attainment. Policy is a tree of which Council is the root, Authority the stem, and Activity the main branch. The seventy-two Prakritis are the leaves; the six qualities of Royalty the blossoms; power and success the flowers and the fruit. Let this shade protect our Gracious Empress for ever.

'And as at the birth of the Great Abkar, which happened at a time when his father's fortunes were fallen so low that he possessed neither crown, nor kingdom, nor even the wherewithal to make the necessary gifts to his friends and followers when a son was born unto him, he took a musk-pod, and breaking it divided it amongst them, uttering the wish that proved a prophecy; so may thy name, most noble Mercia, and thy virtues spread in waves of perfume throughout thy wide domains, making glad the hearts of thy faithful subjects, and filling them with joy, and peace and love.

'May the blessing of the Eternal Father rest upon thee and thine for ever and for ever.'

THE END

PRINTED BY
SPOTTISWOODE AND CO., NEW-STREET SQUARE
LONDON

# IDYLLS, LEGENDS, AND LYRICS.

## By A. GARLAND MEARS.

Portrait.  Superfine paper.  Cloth, gold lettered.  Price **6s**.

---

*NEWCASTLE CHRONICLE.*—'As an Alpine traveller might pluck the eidelweiss in some unexpected cranny, so we open the pages of a volume of IDYLLS, LEGENDS, AND LYRICS. It is the work of a poet of Nature. . . . Mrs. Mears strikes her harp with power and grace, and breathes life and poetry into the dry bones of history.  Interest will be aroused in them, not only by their poetic treatment, but also by the erudition displayed by the author.

'The legends of her volume are enhanced by notes betraying considerable research. . . . Mrs. Mears may be indeed described as the poet of love. . . . She is a close observer of human passion. Never before have we seen such a complete analysis of the tender passion as that given in the series of eighteen sonnets under the title of HONORIA'S LOVE. . . . IDYLLS, LEGENDS, AND LYRICS go into the world with the stamp of approval, and, in winning credit for their author, they reflect honour upon the town that saw their birth.'

*MANCHESTER COURIER.*—'Considerable variety of style and sentiment are illustrated in these interesting verses.  The dramatic Idyll ILAMEA; HONORIA'S LOVE, and other Sonnets; EDAIN, AN ANCIENT LEGEND OF IRELAND; POEMS IN BLANK VERSE; CÆDMON, AN EARLY ENGLISH IDYLL, together with SONGS and LYRICAL POEMS, are all samples of composition which indicate that the author is no novice in such work.  In HONORIA'S LOVE are depicted the several emotions of the mind when under the influence of love, each sonnet expressing a separate phase of that passion which is admitted to be the strongest of all human passions Owing to the form of the verse these eighteen sonnets are less a love story, perhaps, than an exposition of the emotions.  The following is a specimen of them. . . . With one other quotation we will close this admirable book.

### 'LOVE, THE UNIVERSAL LAW.

' As atom unto atom firmly lies
   Obeying blindly that great law which makes
   Subservient even lifeless matter ; wakes
   An energy, a force whose hidden ties
   Bind animate, or inanimate in wise
   True order.   See, the silver cloudlet breaks,
   With others interweaves ; thus changed forsakes
   An individual existence, dies.

' Wave follows wave in rhythmic lines, and one
   By one they lose themselves in close embrace ;
   Thus are we twain commingled : our lives run
   In closest sympathy ; we interlace
   Our mind's emotions : now, there hath begun
   Creation new, to which past life gives place.'

*OXFORD CHRONICLE.*—' This is an 8vo. volume, printed in clear type, on thick paper ; cloth, gilt lettered. Its pages are laden with the music of the love song and old-time love story. The aim of the author, not only to reach the reasoning faculties, but to appeal to the imagination and emotions ; and to yield that pleasure to the mind which is the design of poetry as of music, has been gained. True poetry, it has been said, portrays, with terrible energy, the excesses of the passions ; but they are passions which show a mighty nature ; which are full of power ; which command awe, and excite a deep though shuddering sympathy. Its great tendency and power is to carry the mind above and beyond the beaten, dusty, and weary walks of ordinary life : to lift it into a purer element, and to breathe into it a more profound and generous emotion.  This consummation has been obtained by the dramatic Idyll ILAMEA, with which Part I. opens.  Its sublimity and elegance of style entitle it to rank as one of the finest classics ever written on love.'

*NORTHERN ECHO.*—' IDYLLS, LEGENDS, AND LYRICS bespeak the true poetic vein ; the light phantasy of romantic thought ; and the faculty of expressing all in rhythmic verse.  A Dramatic Idyll, ILAMEA, is, perhaps, the happiest in the volume  It dwells, as really does the whole book, on the immortal theme of love ; and an argumentative colloquy between two persons, the Count and Ilamea, reveals a flow of language and beautifully balanced metre that make it a pleasure to read or recite.'

*DAILY TELEGRAPH.*—'This work is principally composed of old-time love stories in verse, which the author claims have never before formed subject of treatment by the poet. They present a picture, though only a legendary one, of the days of our ancestors, and are interesting on that account. A bouquet of love sonnets are treated with no little skill and originality. An ancient legend of Ireland is very cleverly and sympathetically rendered in EDAIN ; CÆDMON, an Early English Idyll, is also noteworthy. It is something to be reminded of the " peasant poet who, a thousand years before Milton, sang the epic of the Creation : vividly depicting the War in Heaven, the Fall of Satan, and his Counsellings in Hell." The author has produced a collection of poems which exhibit true poetic instinct; and the work makes a goodly and acceptable volume.'

*THE GRAPHIC.*—'The love song and love story form the staple of Mrs. Garland Mears' IDYLLS, LEGENDS, AND LYRICS. She possesses much fluency of expression, and is not troubled in her theme by any melancholy transcendentalism. In her view the object of poetry is to yield pleasure to the mind, and it should appeal either to the imagination or to the emotions. " Its true object," she observes, " is not obtained when it becomes chiefly the vehicle for philosophical or metaphysical instruction reaching only the reasoning faculties." Some of the poems have a simple love tale for their basis, as in ILAMEA, CÆDMON, and THE LOVE OF UTHER, the British King, for Igerna, with the resultant birth of Arthur. In HONOBIA'S LOVE we have a series of eighteen sonnets ; from the first of these we quote the eight opening lines dealing with " Love's Entrance."

> ' " Oh, kingly Love, when first thou didst enthral
> My soul in thy sweet bonds I hardly knew
> Thy presence : filled with joy, what could I do
> But gaze upon thy face, and at thy call
> Give willing ear ? Then straight before thee fall,
> In meekness yielding loving homage, true.
> What sum of bliss wrapped up in moments few ;
> Life's sweetest mystery is made my all ! " '

*Extracts from Letters containing Criticisms by the Chairmen and Secretaries of Public Libraries :—*

'The librarian has handed to me the volume of IDYLLS, LEGENDS, AND LYRICS. I have had time to read the dramatic Idyll ILAMEA, and am greatly pleased with its sweetness and high-souled tone.

'It makes one feel better and stronger for its impressive lesson, so vividly, and pathetically, and sympathetically told. ILAMEA is worth the price of the whole volume.

'I will devote the earliest opportunity to go through its pages, feeling sure that they will add much pleasure to my life, as well as intensify my attachment to poetry. The work is placed in the library of this borough.

'B. P. WRIGHT, J.P.,

'*Chairman of Committee, Free Public*
'*Library, Stafford.*'

'The MAYOR OF SLIGO has requested that a second copy of IDYLLS, LEGENDS, AND LYRICS be purchased. The verses are very sweet. They do not stir the spirit like the strong lines of Byron ; but they come over us with a bewitching softness that in certain moods is still more delightful, and soothe the troubled spirits with a refreshing sense of truth, purity, and elegance.

'They are pensive rather than passionate, and more full of wisdom and tenderness than flights of fancy, or overwhelming bursts of emotion; while they are moulded into grace, at least as much by the effect of the moral beauties they disclose as by the taste and judgment with which they are constructed.

'DAVID SAULTRY,

'*Chief Librarian, Free Public Library,*
'*Sligo, Ireland.*'

' I have read the first poem, ILAMEA, in this interesting volume of verse, and can bear my testimony as to its beauty of conception and true poetic merit. I like the poetry exceedingly, and feel quite confident that the work only requires to be better known to secure it a very wide circulation.

'ALFRED LANCASTER,
' *Chief Librarian, Free Public Library.*
' *St. Helens.*'

'I am very glad to see in IDYLLS, LEGENDS, and LYRICS a poem on Cædmon. I am particularly interested in old-time literature myself, and am giving special attention to such subjects as " Cædmon " and " Beowulf."

' I shall be very glad to have another copy, as it is the first work I have seen for a long time which is so exactly suited to my taste.

'FRED TURNER,
' *Free Public Library, Brentford.*'

' This work is an exceptionally good one, and I thank you for calling my attention to a volume of poems of such merit as these possess.

' I have told my committee that, as far as I am a judge of poetry, I considered that this work was entitled to a place on our shelves.

'Our public here are quick to form fairly accurate opinions as to the value of works of this class. I shall be only too glad to find my own judgment endorsed by that large body I have the pleasure to serve.

'WILLIAM MAY,
' *Chief Librarian, Free Public Library,*
' *Birkenhead.*'

# THE STORY OF A TRUST.

## By the same Author.

### PORTRAIT AND BIOGRAPHICAL NOTICE.

Crown 8vo. 300 pp. cloth, gilt lettered, price 2*s*. 6*d*.

*OXFORD CHRONICLE.*—'The authoress has been designated
"the Poet of Love, and Nature," one who deserves the thanks of
every student of early English literature for reviving one's interest
in old-time literature.  Her claim to the eulogy is fully justified . . .
this latest production of her pen is thoroughly realistic, and contains word-pictures graphically descriptive of English country life.
. . . Margaret is a gem, a perfect type of womanhood, calling forth
love and admiration.  The chapter containing the tragedy is ably
written, and will commend itself to the approval of lovers of the
dramatic; while the chapter on "Sorrow" appeals powerfully to
the emotions.'

*NEWCASTLE CHRONICLE.*—'Deserves a hearty welcome at
the hands of the general public, and especially of North-country
people. . . . Mrs. Garland Mears' style is fluent and forcible; she
avoids all prevalent errors of latter-day writers, and depending
entirely on her own thoughts, which she expresses in good English.'

*SHEFFIELD DAILY TELEGRAPH.*—'The tale is most
interesting and graphically written. . . . Mrs. Garland Mears has
creditably added both in prose and poetry to the literature of the
period.'

*BRADFORD MERCURY.*—'The narrative is vividly told, and
is interspersed with many historical references to Bradford.  Mrs.
Mears is a charming writer, and all her tales are graphically
written.'

*BRADFORD OBSERVER.*—'Considerable dramatic interest
in the stories, and their relation to the West Riding of Yorkshire,
will give them special interest in this neighbourhood.'

*MANCHESTER EXAMINER.*—'The book is interesting
throughout.  The historical chapters dealing with York City and
Hartlepool are admirable.'

*YORKSHIRE POST.*—'The tone of the book is always
admirable.'

www.ingramcontent.com/pod-product-compliance
Lightning Source LLC
Chambersburg PA
CBHW021725110726
47902CB00005B/1350